THE BENSON

AN EXPERIMENT IN TERROR SHORT
STORY #2.5

KARINA HALLE

For my OGs

INTRODUCTION

The Benson is a novella that fits in between Red Fox (#2) and Dead Sky Morning (#3). It can be read as a standalone.

THE BENSON

I HAVE NEVER BEEN INSIDE THE BENSON HOTEL before. Looking back, it's kind of weird since I've lived in Portland for my whole life, but I guess there are a lot of things in your city you never see. Not the way the tourists do.

Tonight though, I decided I would be a tourist. Having a camera at my side would certainly help in that pretense. I smile up at the doorman as I make my way up the sidewalk, pausing briefly at the bronze plaque on the ground as I have many times before when walking throughout downtown, and then timidly walk up the steps inside.

"Good evening and welcome to The Benson ma'am," the doorman says to me, cheery enough in his fancy, gold-gilded uniform. Still, I feel like he's judging me and what I'm wearing; my Doc Martens still muddy from the morning's rainfall, my maroon leggings with a hole in them and a scuffed leather jacket. I'm obviously not a guest here, not at one of the most prestigious hotels in the state of Oregon.

I give him a tight smile and walk past him into the revolving doors which sweep me inside. The lobby is surprisingly busy for nine p.m. as there's a line at the vast checkout counter a few people deep, and the bar/lounge to the right of me is crammed full of swanky patrons swilling martinis. I barely have time to take in the understated grandeur and opulence of the lobby – which totally reminds me of the golden age of Hollywood – before a waving movement brings my attention to the bar again.

In the corner, swilling what can only be a Jack Daniels and Coke is Dex. Actually, he's not swilling it. Rather, downing it in fast gulps and as soon as he sees he's caught my attention, he waves the prim waitress over and orders another one.

I swallow hard, feeling all sorts of strange feelings rush up in my body. I'm nervous, I already was, but I'm excited too and though my breath catches slightly when I see him, it eventually flows out all hot, ragged and sparkling with nerves.

I haven't seen Dex since we parted ways at the airport in Albuquerque. It wasn't long ago, but it still makes me feel like I'm going on a first date all over again. Not that we ever were dating and not that (with his girlfriend Jenn) we ever would. But I can't help the way I feel. Stupid. And in love with my partner.

I smile, broad and completely natural for him, and make my way to where he is sitting, at a small, white clothed table just big enough for two. Before I reach his side, I wonder if he's going to hug me and before I can finish the thought, he stands up, stepping around the table. I am quickly enveloped into his arms. He smells like Old Spice and a bit like the hand-rolled cigarettes he picked up in New Mexico. His arms are strong and firm around my back. The hug is close, tight and genuine. I relax slightly, wishing we were somewhere else and not this busy lounge where people watch us with disinterest.

I am the first to pull apart, though I could have stayed in his arms all night. I give him the once over now that I am up close.

He looks pretty much as he did in New Mexico. The cuts on his face from the shapeshifter's attack are faded; his moustache has been trimmed, almost gone, as is the scruff beard under his chin. His eyebrow ring glints from his black brow. His cheekbones are high, perhaps higher than before. I take another step back and see that he's lost a little bit of weight. It shows in his face most of all.

"Checking me out again?" he says, his voice low, his lips snaking to the side in a smirk. There's something off about him, but I don't know what it is. Maybe it's because, despite the closeness of the hug, there's an awkward distance between us, like we aren't sure how to act around each other now that the skinwalkers and Maximus and sharing a bed for a few nights are gone. We both almost died in New Mexico – I know it had an impact on us, but it doesn't seem to have any bearing here in the swanky Benson hotel.

And then there are his eyes. Dex's eyes are his focal point, the part of him that wins people over or drives them away. Dark chocolate, enigmatic and emotive. Sometimes they are ruthless, sometimes seductive. They are a mystery as much as he is and the one thing I can't help from drowning in over and over again.

But here, tonight, they are clouded. No, that's not quite it. Not clouded but subdued. The sparkle and zest that roam in them, no matter what his mood, are gone. They are handsome, beguiling eyes but not his.

I think back to Red Fox and how he had gone so long without his anti-psychotic medication that he began to actually feel again. It was scary for him, no doubt (and for me, let's not kid ourselves) but in the end...he was free. Or so I thought. Now it seems that sparkle and life, the manic highs and lows, are gone. As destructive as they were, they are an important part of him.

"Sorry," I mutter to myself, dropping my eyes quickly to the table just as the waitress comes by and puts down his drink.

"What would you like, Perry?" he asks me. I look up at him and the waitress. Her name tag states her as Prudence. She has white hair and a friendly smile but a stance that says I better be quick with an answer.

I don't drink normally, especially not on the job – which is what I am doing here tonight with Dex – but I say, "A glass of the house red, thanks."

It's the cheapest and will relax my nerves. Prudence leaves with my order after Dex gives her a quick wink. He then turns to me as we sit down.

"So how are you, kiddo?" he asks, peering at my face, trying to read me before I say anything. "Is it nice having me in your neck of the woods again?"

"It's just nice to see you again," I say honestly. With Dex living in Seattle and me in Portland, I only ever see him when we film. And in the between time, I miss him.

A blush starts to creep up my neck. I can feel it.

He gives me a smile that reaches his eyes and shows perfect teeth that are quite white for a smoker. "Well, it's nice to see you. Too bad you're not bunking with me tonight at my motel."

I give him a sharp look, not sure if he's kidding or not.

He smiles again, almost leering. "I'll probably be shaking in my boots after tonight with only my pillow to hug."

The waitress comes back and gives me my wine. He gives her the same kind of smirk. This is how I know he's messing with me.

I roll my eyes. "So what is our plan for tonight anyway? Are we just going to sit here and drink and wait for the ghosts to show up?"

"Patience, Perry," he says and takes another gulp of his drink. He gestures to the wine and nods at it. "Have some of that and relax."

I take a sip of the acidic merlot and look around me. As gorgeous and old-fashioned as the hotel is, there are so many people about, and I can't imagine how on earth the place could be haunted. But apparently it is. In fact, Portland has a few ghost tours that come around and poke their heads in the hotel a few times a week. I doubt anybody ever sees anything, though.

"Are we the first ghost hunting show to come inside here?" I ask Dex.

He coughs on his drink and shakes his head. "Fuck no. We're a bit behind on this one. I think just about every ghost hunter has been in this hotel at some point or another."

"Do they ever find anything?"

He gives me a wry look. "What do you think? Of course not."

"What makes you think we will?"

He smiles again and reaches over with his hand to pat me softly on the head. "Because I've got you, kiddo. You're my little ghost bait."

I think back to Red Fox, to a moment when Dex said I might be offered up as bait to the skinwalkers. The idea bothered me then and it bothers me now. I take a longer sip of the wine this time.

He's watching my face closely, as usual, and he still

keeps his hand there. I'm not sure if he's trying to comfort me or what. I shoot him a deadly look from the side of my eyes.

"I'm joking you know," he finally says, his voice less rough, less gravely. "I just mean, well, you know there's something about you, something that attracts these things. You're like a secret weapon."

"Some weapon," I scoff and look down into the glass, my vision becoming a blur of deep reds. "What's the point of just attracting these...things? These people? If I could use this...power...whatever it is, for good...that would be a different story."

He shrugs and takes his hand away, his attention back to his own drink. The back of my head feels vulnerable without his hand there. "You never know. There's supposed to be a shitload of ghosts in this hotel, maybe you can help one of them."

I raise my brows at him.

"A shitload?" I repeat. "Where do you get your information, Mr. Foray?"

"Wikipedia. That thing is never wrong," he says without irony. He looks around him and takes in the scene. "We're supposed to meet the night manager, Pam, in a couple of minutes. She said she'd find us. She'll give us a tour of the place; hopefully give us the real story. I want that on film."

"And what do you want me to do?" I ask. Once again, we're going into a film shoot more or less blind. And by we, I mean I. Dex always knows what's going on and I'm always in the dark. I did research The Benson before biking over here and all that, but I have no clue what to do or say. There is no storyboard, no script. We just wing it and I usually end up looking like an idiot.

"Just be yourself. Ask her questions. I'll film both of you. We'll wander around the hotel. Then we'll probably be allowed to go off on our own and do some exploring. I'll give you the infrared camera this time so we can see if we pick up any hot or cold spots."

I shiver at that thought. Using the infrared meant we'd be wandering around in the dark. Whether I'm in a lighthouse on the coast or in the New Mexican desert, the darkness still gives me the creeps. Especially now that I know there are things out there that want to hurt me. That know I'm a sort of "bait."

By the time Pam shows up, I have finished my glass of wine. It has only left me anxious, not relaxed.

Pam is on the overweight side, similar to the way I was in high school, but unlike me, she seems to bustle with confidence. Or bustle with something. Her wide, cheery face gives her the appearance of being younger than she probably is and she speaks a mile a minute.

"You must be Perry and Dex, I recognized you!" she exclaims, beaming at us and holding out her hand. We both give it a quick shake. She points to the name tag on her black suit. "As you can see, my name is Pam. Pam Gupta. I'm the night manager here at The Benson."

"Thanks for having us," Dex tells her sincerely, reaching under the table and bringing out a backpack and a camera bag.

"No, thank you," she says putting extra emphasis on the words. "As soon as you told me who you were, I looked up your ghost show and immediately fell in love with you guys."

Dex and I exchange a quick look.

"I mean," she corrects herself and lets out an awkward clip of a laugh, "I was scared witless at the Darkhouse episode and the one in Red Fox but I was so drawn in by you two. You're just so...so..."

"Handsome?" Dex asks, flashing her a smile and stroking his chin scruff.

She blushes and giggles. "Well, yeah I guess you are."

I roll my eyes. Dex doesn't need any more encouragement.

"But," she continues, "you're both just so...lucky!"

We look at each other again, even more confused.

"Lucky?" I ask.

"How about I explain as we walk? I don't have much time to show you around before I start my shift."

We get up, Dex giving the backpack of equipment to me, and we follow Pam through the lobby. For a larger woman she walks like a sprite, moving quickly between people and showering her big smile on all of them. The guests eye Dex and I curiously, intrigued by the camera he has placed up on his shoulder.

We stop before a grand staircase leading up to the second floor. I eye myself quickly in the mirror on the landing. My floral dress is sticking to my leggings in static cling, and my black hair is a mess from my motorbike helmet (and Dex's hand). I don't look camera worthy at all. I shrug helplessly at my reflection and look to Pam who is pointing up at the stairs.

"There's been many sightings of one of ghostly guests walking up and down this very staircase," she says, sounding like a chipper tour guide talking about museum pieces and not dead people.

I look at Dex beside me and see the camera is going, picking up everything Pam is saying. Sensing I'm staring at him, he reaches out and pushes me toward Pam, into the frame. I know he wants me to start acting like the host I am.

I smooth down my hair and clear my throat, stepping into the shot. "Have you seen any ghosts, Pam?"

She shakes her head quickly and looks wistful. "No, I haven't. Come on, let's go to the next floor."

Not exactly the answer I was hoping for.

She scurries up the stairs and we follow, my short legs straining to keep up with her quick busybody motion.

We walk toward the elevators and as we are waiting she says, "I think you two are lucky because I've always wanted to see a ghost. I believe in them. So badly. But I've never seen one. Weird, right, considering that I run The Benson. At night."

The elevator dings and the doors open. There's a couple inside who eye the camera with trepidation, but we step inside with them anyway. Pam makes small talk with them as she pushes the button for the 8th floor and doesn't mention ghosts again until the couple get out at the 5th floor.

She tilts her head at us. "I don't like to discuss the ghosts around the guests though. People can be pretty strange about things like that."

"I don't blame them," I find myself saying.

"I guess you'd know," Pam says as the elevator stops at the floor, and she leads us out into the hallway, past a rotary phone resting on top of an antique table.

She notices me eyeing it and gives it a quick wave with her hand. Her bracelets jingle with the motion.

"We try to keep all the original furnishings from the hotel. Adds to the class and elegance of the place, don't you think?"

I nod, not really needing to be sold on the hotel as a whole.

Pam takes us to the right, and we walk past the rooms

down to the very end of the hall. Dex keeps filming, even though he takes his head away from the camera.

"So, if we show The Benson in a good way," Dex says to Pam, "any chance we can score a free hotel room for the night? I'm staying at a roach motel outside of the city, and I'm getting itchy just thinking about it."

Pam turns around briefly and smiles at him but then spins around and keeps walking without missing a beat.

"We'll see. Would you two be sharing the room?"

Dex automatically grins and looks down at me as we walk. I shake my head, not amused.

"No, Perry snores and kicks in her sleep," he says.

I smack him on the shoulder and the camera shakes.

"I do not!" I protest.

"Oh, and drools," he adds quickly.

"So you two are a couple?" Pam asks, not looking at us this time but slowing down as she nears the end of the hall.

"Only in certain situations," I mutter under my breath.

"No, we are not. Perry is far too good for me and I am forced to make do with my Wine Babe girlfriend."

Finally Pam stops walking and looks at him. "Wine Babe? You're with someone from that show?"

"You've seen it?" Dex asks, his eyes wide and hopeful.

"Yes," she says slowly, and for once her chipper look is gone. Her cheeks sag a bit. "My ex boyfriend used to drool all over that skinny, exotic one."

"Yeah, that's his girlfriend. Jennifer Rodriguez," I inform her. She eyes me and sees that I'm none too thrilled about it either. Nothing like a hot woman to make two chubby girls feel like they're having a bonding moment.

"Well, I'm just glad some women watch it," Dex says, turning his attention the camera, perhaps feeling the animosity and low self-esteem just reeking from our pores.

Pam laughs and the cheery façade returns. "Don't be silly. I don't watch that dreadful show. They pair shiraz with Kraft Dinner. Only an idiot would watch that. Like my ex-boyfriend."

Dex opens his mouth to say something, but I know he completely agrees. That's the reason he quit doing camera work on Wine Babes and started up Experiment in Terror with me instead.

"Anyway," she continues, "here we are."

I look at the door we've stopped in front of: Room 818.

"Where are we?" I ask.

"This was Parker's room," she says ominously.

"Who is Parker?" Dex asks. I'm surprised that he doesn't know something for once.

"Parker..." Pam starts and then trails off. She takes her keys out from her pocket; the noise of them rattling fills the hallway. It suddenly seems very empty and hollow and a weird, familiar feeling washes over me, causing the hairs on the back of my neck to stand up.

The lock turns, and the door slowly creaks open. Only blackness and dust come billowing out of the room.

"After you," Pam says.

Dex shrugs and then nudges me in front of the camera, indicating that I am to go first. Of course. I always have to be the first to walk into everything when I'm on camera. And sometimes when I'm not on camera. It depends on how sadistic Dex is feeling.

I take in a deep breath and push the door aside. It slowly swings open with a low groan, and I walk blindly into the swirling dark.

"Should I be putting on the night vision?" Dex asks no one in particular. I hear him fiddle with the camera settings but before anything happens, I am blind. Pam has walked in beside me and switched on the lights.

"No sense in scaring ourselves yet," she chirps, and I can barely make out her round face.

Dex comes in and Pam shuts the door behind him. Once my eyes adjust to the light, I see that we are in a hotel room that probably looks the same as any other hotel room, albeit a large and very pricey one. Aside from a heavy chill that seems to hang in the air, there's nothing too off-putting about the place. The bed is made, there seems to be a separate room with a living area, divided only by a Japanese-type paper partition, and I can just see a rather opulent looking bathroom jutting out to the right.

"As I said, this is Parker's room," she says. "Well, it was his room. I say this because some guests who stay in here say they still see him. But it happens very rarely."

"And once again," Dex repeats, sounding bored, "who is Parker?"

Pam walks over to the king-sized bed and sits down on it. It sags a little from her weight; the mattress is not as springy as it was back in the day.

"We have a lot of ghosts in this hotel. Parker isn't the most well known of them, but he is the most real. Because he was a real person and his story is terribly tragic. Tragic, but all too common."

I go over to the bed and sit down beside Pam. Suddenly, that slightly see-through partition between the bedroom and the living area is giving me the creeps, like I can sense someone standing behind it.

Dex looks like he picks up on the vibe too. Although he is standing in front of Pam and I, with the camera in our faces, his eyes keep flitting over there and his head is cocked slightly as if he is listening. I stifle the urge to shiver—I don't want to look like an amateur—and keep my attention on Pam.

"What happened?" I ask, trying to keep my voice light, trying to ignore the goosebumps I can feel rising underneath my jacket.

"Parker, Parker Hayden, was a ship owner in the '30s. Back then, Portland was a very different city. The ships were its lively hood. There was a lot of money, a lot of crime, a lot of... well, scandals, I guess. Think Vegas, but on a river. Anyway, Parker was just one of the many wealthy ship owners. He spent half his time here, half somewhere on the east coast. He rented a room, this room, spending an obscene amount of money every night. He was a ladies man too, no surprise there! He was also a bit nuts. But because he was rich, you called him eccentric. There were rumors he was having an affair with a maid or two; sometimes he'd be caught stealing tons of toiletries and hording them in his closet. In this day and age we'd call him a weirdo but back then, he was just rich and powerful and you let him do what he wanted."

"Doesn't sound too much different from nowadays," Dex says softly, keeping the camera focused on Pam. He's paying less attention now to the other room, which makes me feel a smidge better.

Pam laughs. "You're right about that. And it was the same kind of outcome. Back in 1934, Portland was hit hard —really hard—with this strike. I think it was called the West Coast Waterfront Strike? Anyway, there was the strike, his ship was basically inoperable, and he lost a lot of money. Really fast. According to the records, he was kicked out of the hotel because he couldn't pay his bills. Not for this room, not for any room here."

"And what happened?" I push.

She sighs and rubs her face quickly, looking uneasy for the first time tonight. Lines appear on her youthful face.

"He wouldn't leave. He was kicked out several times, out on the street even. Publicly humiliated. All unshaven and messy, like a vagrant. He said people were after him, wanting money and that he was afraid for his life. Then the hotel staff found him. Dead. Hanging in the maid's laundry room, from a noose made out of towels. The strike ended two days later. How is that for irony?"

She smiles at me, but it is forced and I can't be bothered to return it. The story stirs something in my gut.

I look up at Dex and see that his attention is back on the other room again.

"What is it?" I ask him. I can't help myself.

Pam's attention goes to him, and we all look over but see nothing.

"The guests who have seen him," she puts in, her voice low, her eyes on the partition, "they say they see a man pacing anxiously in the other room there, muttering to himself. Once he notices you, he tries to say something or write something down. But no words come out and as the guests get more scared and confused, the ghost gets frustrated. Sometimes he disappears, sometimes he rushes at the guests and then... poof."

"Well doesn't that make for a memorable stay," Dex comments underneath his breath.

Pam giggles nervously at his lame joke and then gets up. "I'm afraid I will have to leave you two now. Duty calls."

Dex lowers the camera and touches her arm lightly, causing her to pause mid-bustle. It's obvious she wants nothing more than to get out of the room. I have half a mind to join her.

"Where is the laundry room?" he asks.

Pam looks down at her feet quickly. "The laundry room? Why?"

"Well, we aren't ignoring the place where the man hung himself. With towels, mind you. I mean, I can make a swan out of towels, but a noose?"

"I'd show you, but I really must—"

She looks at me for support as he reaches forward and plucks the keys out of her hand.

He holds up the keys in front of her face. "Just tell us which key will get us into the laundry room and we'll have no problem finding it on our own."

"Dex," I begin, not wanting him to step out of bounds. He can be relentless sometimes.

He ignores me and flashes Pam a smile that usually makes me weak at the knees. "Come on, Pammy, you know you want our little show to succeed here. Parker would want us there. Give the man some closure."

Her mouth twitches while she thinks it over. Dex gives her a quick wink and she blushes slightly. I can't help but roll my eyes again.

"All right," Pam mumbles and takes the keys from him. She goes through them in a blur and pops one off the ring and into his outstretched hand. "It's in the basement. This will open the freight elevator at the end of the hall and take you right there. But I want this back, OK?"

"But of course." He grins and closes his hand over the key before she has a chance to change her mind.

She looks at me and I give a little shrug.

"We won't wreck anything or scare the guests," I say. I want to add, "We promise," but I know we can't promise anything. Destruction and fear seem to follow Dex and I wherever we go. That is the nature of the ghost hunting business, even one that's only on the Internet.

I can see Pam isn't comfortable with the situation, but she doesn't say anything else. She just leaves the room and shuts the door behind her. The movement causes the dust to fly off of the nearby lamps.

I slowly let out my breath and look at Dex. He's watching me carefully.

"What?" I ask.

"Do you want the lights on or off?"

He raises his camera a bit and I get it. Are we going to shoot this in the dark or in the light? I know what I'm going to say, and I know what he's going to say.

"Leave the lights on," I tell him.

"I think we should have them off."

I knew it. "Why do you even bother consulting me if you're just going to do what you want anyway?"

"I like you to feel like this a partnership," he says, and sounds strangely sincere. He tucks the key into his cargo pants and gives me a quick smile. "And you know that shooting in the dark adds to the tension."

"It also adds to my ever-building threat of dying young," I point out.

"Twenty-two ain't so young anymore, kiddo. I mean, you've almost surpassed James Dean. If you kick it now—"

I raise my hand in the air. "That's enough. Let's just get this over with."

"Perry's famous last words."

"Dex. Shut up."

It's his turn to roll his eyes. I feel a cold waft come in from the living room area, and I automatically rub my hands up and down my arms. There's definitely something going on in this place, and I am in no hurry to find out. But of course, it's my job to find out.

"What if we just leave this light on here?" I say,

pointing at the lamp. The rest of hotel room, including the bathroom and the living area, are only lit by residual light. It's just dark enough to be spooky over there, but it's not so black that I'd be having a panic attack.

"If you wish," Dex says and I hate how unafraid he sounds. Then again, he always gets to view things through the lens. He never has to be the one seeing the horrors face-to-face.

It's a catch-22 with my job. On one hand, I'm often scared shitless at the slightest thing and pray that I don't bump into a ghost (or a skinwalker, now that I know those things exist). On the other hand, if I don't run into anything, it makes for a pretty bad episode. I mean, most ghost hunting shows don't have much to show for themselves, anyway, but that's also the point: We don't want to be like most of those shows. We are above and beyond that, at least that's what Dex rattles off half the time. I don't even know if he believes what he says, but the fact is that when we do capture some unexplainable stuff on film, the views go up and we look good.

It's too bad our looking good comes at the cost of me nearly peeing my pants every time.

"So..." I begin.

"So, just come here." He places his strong hands on the sides of my arms and physically moves me over so I'm right in front of him and the camera. I don't want him to let go but he does. "I'll roll it, you give a quick spiel based on whatever Pam just said and then walk into the other room. I'll be right behind you."

"Don't I get a flashlight?"

"I'll be your eyes. Ready?"

I nod, square my shoulders and take a deep breath. We usually go in just one take and I give a very quick overview of what we are doing in The Benson hotel and what we hope to find in room 818.

Then I turn around and face the darkness of the living room. I don't know how it's possible, but it seems to have grown darker in the last few minutes. Before I could make out a couch and a table, as well as the entrance to the fancy bathroom. Now, I can't see anything at all. Just the partition with its slightly transparent sheets of fabric paper and that terrible feeling that there is something, or someone, just beyond it, waiting for me to enter its clutches.

Dex clears his throat, a signal that I need to move. I feel frozen on the spot but will my legs to step forward, even though every part of me is screaming not to.

Somehow, I do it. I step into the void and feel a rush of frigid air flow around me. No, flow is too gentle of a word. It slams into me like an invisible hand.

I pause and take another step, trying to pick up where the bed should be. I still can't see anything, but Dex says in a low voice, "Move to the right a little. The bed is right in front of you."

I do as he says and stop. Dex sucks in his breath in one sharp motion.

"What is it?" I whisper uneasily. I wish I could see what he is seeing.

"Do you not see it?"

I turn around and see his silhouette against the light. "See what?" I feel the symptoms of a panic attack poking around my spine.

He doesn't say anything but keeps the camera trained on me while reaching into his backpack. He pulls out what looks like the small infrared camera.

"Here, turn the switch on, it's on the side," he says and hands it to me. I fumble for it, feeling around for the button.

It comes on and then I can see again. Well, kind of. It's aimed at the floor and I can see the shape of my feet and legs glowing a hot red against the blackness. I feel a lot like I'm in Predator.

"Now turn around and aim it straight in front of you."

I hesitate for a second, afraid of what I'm going to witness. Then I turn on the spot so I'm facing the black room and look through the infrared camera.

I nearly drop it.

Right in front of me, to the side of the bed, is a tall, long shape of pale blue light. A hazy silhouette. The outline of a man who isn't there.

"That's unbelievable," I hear Dex say from behind me. I can't form the words to agree. The fear is overpowering my fascination. There is someone standing right in front of me. Parker Hayden.

"Talk to it."

"What?" I whisper hoarsely, my eyes flitting from the screen to the blackness in front of me. If I walk forward, will my hands grab onto a desperate dead man? Or will they pass through them, like no one is there at all? Do I even want to know?

"Mr. Hayden," Dex speaks in a gentle voice, void of any self-consciousness. "Mr. Hayden, we can see you. Would you like to talk to us? Would you like to tell us something?"

The shape on the camera shakes vigorously on the spot, like the picture on a television that's being hit from the side. Then it stops and in a blink of an eye it bursts out of the screen, screaming past us in a blur of cold, miserable energy.

And just like that, all the lights in the room come on and it's just Dex and I left staring at each other, cameras in hand, feeling cold and dumbfounded at what we just encountered.

I manage to shut my mouth so I don't look like a drooling fool on camera and look back down at the infrared.

"We need to follow him."

I look up at Dex with the most incredulous stinkeye I can muster.

"We need to follow him? We don't even know what that was. Or who that was. Or where he went. Or if he wants us to follow him..."

Dex turns around and heads to the door.

"Dex!" I yell after him and grab onto his sleeve. I look up at his eyes but I can see he's already gone, thinking in the mind of a ghost, plotting where Parker would have gone next.

"Perry, we can't just leave it at that."

"I don't know, I think what we just captured is some pretty awesome stuff. Maybe that's all we'll get for tonight. Maybe it's time to go home."

The side of his mouth twitches and before I know it, he's grinning at me. "Why Perry, I thought you'd turned into quite the little fearless ghost hunter back in Red Fox. Getting cold feet, are we?"

I wish I had a snappy rebuttal for that, but I don't. The truth is, I'm scared. It doesn't matter how many times you've seen a ghost; it's still scary. And considering how often these supernatural beings have tried to kill me in the past, I think I have every right to fear each one I encounter. Every chance I get to get out of the shoot alive is a chance I want to take. I mean, deep down inside, I'm just an ordinary, 22-year-old girl who likes to listen to metal and dreams about chocolate on a nightly basis. Just because I'm ghost bait, doesn't mean I have to exploit it.

But I don't say any of this to Dex. Even though he's just my partner (and I'm usually the sane one), I can't bear the thought of losing face with him. He took a risk by creating this show and by putting me in it. I took a risk by giving up my old job to make something of my life. I want to be the person that he thinks I am, that fearless, brave girl—woman, even—who laughs in the face of danger. Something more than ordinary.

"Cold feet?" I repeat, my voice hard. "You're the one who is showing up all icy on my infrared."

He studies me for a second, sucking slowly on his full lower lip, trying to read me. I hate it when he does that. But instead of looking away as I often do, I hold his gaze, challenging him.

"OK, kiddo. Glad to see you're still up for the challenge," he finally says.

"I deal with you every weekend, don't I? Anything after that is a piece of cake."

He flashes me a quick smile and opens the door. I follow him into the hallway, take in a deep breath and try to calm my nerves, which are firing all over the place and causing me to shake internally. My bluff worked. Now all I need to do is keep up appearances.

As we walk down the hallway to the freight elevator, I already know where Dex is planning on taking us: the laundry room. I don't want to think about the horrors that might lie there, so I ask him, "You told me you saw something, before I turned on the infrared... what was it?"

We stop in front of the elevator and Dex inserts the key, giving it a turn and pressing the down button. The elevator purrs loudly, as if it hasn't been turned on in decades. I'm reminded of The Shining for a brief instance and hope a river of blood doesn't come flowing out of it.

"Just some really weird lights dancing around. You know how you can get those orbs on screen, like the ones we saw at the lighthouse? Same kind of thing but they were jumping up and down, like balls in a lotto machine or something."

The elevator button light goes off, and with a loud metallic groan, the doors slide open to expose a larger than average elevator behind them.

"Ladies first," Dex says, but I shove him forward. Not this time.

We get in and press the button for the laundry level, which is marked, thankfully. It's also below the first floor and the first two parking levels, which is a slight cause for concern. Just how far down are we going?

I give Dex a nervous smile, which he returns with a mischievous one. An agonizing minute later, we lurch to a stop on the laundry level.

The doors shudder slightly, then open as if being pried by invisible hands. In front of us lies a long hallway, poorly lit by buzzing overhead lights, casting shadows on the few doors that lie along the way. Not the most welcoming place.

Dex steps out first. He grabs my hand, his grasp on mine firm and warm, and I let myself feel the momentary wash of comfort that only he can provide for me. I let him lead me into the hallway. The elevator doors remain open and waiting for the next passenger, only on this empty, quiet floor, there is none to be found.

Dex hoists the camera onto his shoulder again and motions for me to turn on the infrared.

"Might as well start filming this now."

"Where is everyone?" I ask. "I mean, the hotel runs around the clock, doesn't it?"

"But which clock?" he answers in a statement, not a question.

I sigh and flip on the infrared again. My body glows a

vibrant red but when I aim it over at Dex, he only comes up orange.

"What?" he asks as I purse my lips, thinking.

"Seems I'm a lot more hot-blooded than you are," I say and quickly show him the screen, placing his hand in front of the lens.

He chews on his lip briefly and then places his hand against my forehead. It feels cool.

"Well you're not hot..."

I shoot him a wry look.

"I mean, not internally hot. Outside is another matter." He winks at me.

"Are you flirting with me again, Mr. Foray?"

"Again? Whatever do you—"

He's interrupted by a wall of sound as all doors down the hallway suddenly swing open and bang against their walls. Simultaneously, the elevator behind us powers up with a thunderous whir, the doors closing quickly.

"It's go time," he says and we're off down the hallway to the first door.

Dex is just about to enter the room when the door slams shut in his face, almost smashing his nose back into his skull. He gives me a scared look I don't see on him too often. Probably the thought of having to get a nose job.

He goes for the handle and I'm right there at his side as he jangles it back and forth vigorously. It's locked.

We dash for the next door and the same thing happens. Same with the last door after that. All doors locked. Nothing to explore.

"Now what?" I mumble, feeling a familiar wave of cold snake around my feet and ankles. I point the infrared down at it, but it doesn't register anything out of the ordinary.

Dex doesn't say anything for awhile so I look up at him.

His eyes are focused above him, at a loose-looking vent on the ceiling.

"Perry," he says slowly, carefully.

I shake my head. "You've got to be kidding."

He looks back at me and shrugs. "What's the harm? I'll just boost you up there. If you crawl around for a bit, you'll probably end up in one of the other rooms and then you can open the door from the inside."

"I...don't even know what to say to that."

"No? You usually have some sort of witty one-liner."

"You go up there, Dex. There's no way in hell I'm going."

"You can't hold me up and it's too far for me to jump. Short man syndrome, remember?"

"You can't hold me up."

"Perry, for the last time, stop acting like you weigh one million pounds. You don't. You're as light as a feather."

I let out a laugh. I can't help myself.

"I'm not...anyway, even if you could push me up there, do you think I'd fit?"

"Again, Perry–"

"And if I do get up there, do you think that aging duct would hold me? I'd come crashing through like a bag of bricks."

"Stop using your non-existent weight problem as an excuse, just because you're too chickenshit," he challenges.

My mouth drops slightly. I am not chickentshit. And my weight problem isn't non-existent.

"Fine," I say and walk toward him. "If you don't think it's an issue, then away I go."

He steadies his gaze at me, sussing me out. I cross my arms and give him an impatient stare.

He nods quickly and lowers his hands joined together. I

step on them unsteadily and before I can even question just what the hell I am doing, I'm boosted into the air, one hand on the camera, the other reaching for the vent.

Once Dex has me steadied and I can stand, albeit wobbly, on his hands, I climb to his shoulders and push the vent aside. It pops up and slides out to the side with an easy clatter that rattles down the hallway. Up close, it is big enough for me to fit through. But it's also black and fathomless and hides a wealth of things that could frighten me to death. It's a vent, for crying out loud. Since when did this show turn into Mission Impossible?

"You OK, kiddo?" he asks from beneath me, his voice shaking slightly, either from apprehension or from the strain.

"Not really. Have you ever been in a dark vent before?"

"Several times," he answers seamlessly. "Once you get up in there, I'll hand you the flashlight so you don't have to be in the dark."

"How thoughtful of you," I mutter and reach for my hands into the vent. It's cold and I fear it will be icky inside but the bottom of the duct feels mercifully dry.

"On the count of three," he says and once we count down, he pushes me up further and I'm waist deep. I feel his hands slip away and with a groan I pull myself forward until everything except my calves are inside the dark air duct.

I'm scared as hell. The sides of the duct have me unable to turn around and I can't see what's in front of me. For all I know, there could be a giant rat in front of my face, ready to gnaw it off, starting with the little tip of my nose. I am starting to panic and an attack in this tight of a spot would be a dangerous thing indeed.

"Uh, Perry," I hear Dex say. His voice is comforting but the tone isn't.

"What?" I say as quietly as I can. My words reverberate around me.

"I guess you can't turn around and reach for the flashlight...can you?"

I close my eyes and let my head thud against the cold bottom. "No."

"That's OK, I'm just going to stick the flashlight inside your boot. That way, when you get a chance to move around a bit more, you can grab it."

I feel him grab my leg, undo the laces on my left Doc Marten and shove the flashlight inside.

This has to be the stupidest idea ever. Some ghost hunters we are.

I sigh and then cough loudly from all the dust.

"Perry, I'm going to try and talk you through it. Just move forward until I tell you to stop. And when I tell you to stop, see if there's an opening off to your right. If there is, go down that way and it should place you in the laundry room. At least, I hope it's the laundry room."

"OK!" I yell, hoping my voice will scare off any hideous creatures that are waiting for me up ahead.

You can do this, I tell myself. One movement at a time, like a snake. Remember if you need to escape, you just need to back up and you'll be free.

I repeat this to myself as I slink forward, feeling more and more like Tom Cruise. Or Garth from Wayne's World when he keeps landing on his keys.

After what feels like a lifetime of wiggling and trying to refrain from vomiting on the infrared, Dex yells for me to look for a space going off to the right. I feel for it but though

I still touch the same cold metal walls, there's a bit of a breeze up ahead, flowing down the right side of me.

I continue, hearing Dex's babbling from below becoming more and more muffled, until my hand doesn't slam against the side as normal. I found the opening.

I take it, maneuvering like a rat in a maze and wiggle down in a new direction. After a few beats, I can't hear Dex at all anymore and that realization fills me with dread. If I need to get out, I'll have to not only back up but make a turn going backwards as well. In the pitch dark, the idea is terrifying and disorienting.

But I continue because I'm determined to see this through. And soon enough, my eyes start to pick up something ahead of me. There's just a little difference of light up ahead and then my hands come across cool air and a vent covering.

My fingers wrap around the metallic grate and pull it up with ease. It rattles as I push it to the side and I stick my head down below, taking in deep breaths of fresher, non-contained air through my nose. I don't know what's below me, all I can see are a few red lights, which I guess are the on-off buttons of machines. There is some other light, though, spilling in from under a doorframe and with hope I realize that Dex and the hallway must be on the other side of that.

I carefully slide across the opening, distributing my weight on each side until I'm just past it, then I lower myself down, my legs dangling helplessly. I have no idea what the hell is below me but I'm just going to have to hope for the best. I take a deep breath, wiggle myself out until I'm hanging what must be a good few feet off the ground, and let go.

I land on solid ground, though the impact makes me

stumble to the side and my body goes flying against a desk that makes an impression in my hip.

"Fuck!" I yell. That's going to leave a giant bruise.

"Perry?" I hear Dex call out from the hallway. I scurry over to the door, careful not to trip over anything in my way, and feel for the doorknob. I yank at it to open, but nothing happens. It appears to be locked from the inside and the outside.

"Are you OK?" he asks and I can hear the worry in his voice. He likes to surprise me by acting human from time to time.

"I'm fine," I say, rubbing my hip where the desk went into me. "But I can't open this fucking thing."

"Are you getting any reception on your phone?"

I tuck the infrared under my arm and bring my iPhone out of my jacket pocket, while reaching down for the flashlight in my boot. It works but the bars are gone. No service.

"No, are you?"

"No," he answers with a sigh. "Look, I've been trying the key she gave me and it won't open any of the doors here. I can't call her either. There are some stairs at the end beside the elevator. I'm just going to run up to the lobby and grab Pam."

"Dex, don't you dare leave me!" I yell and pound on the door for impact.

"Well what the hell do you suppose we do then? Hang out like this until a maid shows up? What if they are done for the night? Do you really want to spend a night locked in there?"

No. I don't. But I don't want him taking off and leaving me alone in this scary, dark room either.

"Look," he continues, "I'll be right back. And I mean, right back. I'm not going to let anything happen to you."

That's kind of hard to do when you aren't here, I think but I know I have no choice. Either he goes or I'm locked in here all night. That thought is too terrifying to fathom.

"OK," I say hesitantly.

He taps the door lightly. "I'll be right back."

I hear his feet scurry off and a door at the end of the hall open. And then silence again.

I put my back against the door and face the darkness of the foreign room. I flick the flashlight on and slowly graze it across the black.

In a creepy, fleeting light it illuminates a few laundry bins, laundry machines, a makeshift office consisting of a whiteboard, a file cabinet and the desk I ran into.

And a dead man hanging from the ceiling.

I scream bloody murder, dropping the flashlight and camera in the process.

They fall to my feat in an outburst as loud as my wail, and as I quickly fumble for them, the light in the room goes on.

I raise my hand to my eyes to shield them from the light and try to get a glimpse of what's going on. The image of that dead, bloated man hanging by his neck is seared into my brain.

The laundry hampers, machines and office are all still here.

The hanging man is gone.

There is an African-American woman who stands to my far left, her hand on a light fixture, giving me a quizzical stare. She's young and thin with large eyes and is wearing a plain grey dress with a white ruffled apron across it. A very classic-looking maid.

"Good heavens, child," she exclaims in a thick Southern accent. "What on earth are you doing in here?"

I blink hard, trying to make sense of the situation. The maid looks at my hands and what I'm holding.

"Are you filming me? Who are you? What is this?" she demands, her voice growing higher with each question.

"I...I'm Perry Palomino," I stammer, my voice squeaking.

"Am I supposed to know who you are?" she asks and puts her hands on her hips.

"Uh, no," I say and give her an awkward smile. "I'm here with my partner Dex. Dex Foray. We are, uh, we doing a project here. We have permission of the night manager. Pam...something. She said we could come down here and film."

"Just what are you filming. Charlie Chaplin?"

Hmmmm. How to explain the next part without seeming batshit crazy.

"Well..." I begin.

She cocks her brow at me and folds her arms. She's in no hurry.

I let out a burst of air through my nose and say, "We're ghost hunters."

She smiles, her teeth blindingly white. She doesn't sound as amused as she looks. "You're pulling my chain."

"No, no sadly I'm not. We have a show, Experiment in Terror. It's on the Internet."

"The Internet?"

"I know, it sounds lame but we've been doing quite well. I mean, we have advertisers and people actually tune into watch us. Well, watch me. Since I'm the host. Just not a very good one. Actually I think people tune into laugh at me, but whatever gets me a pay check." I'm rambling now.

"This is a radio show?" she asks.

"No, just on the web."

She frowns and walks toward me, eying my hands. "What kind of camera is that?"

Though there is nothing menacing at all in her voice, I flinch a little and back up into the door. She pauses and gives me another disbelieving look.

"You never seen a black woman before?"

"Huh?"

"I know we aren't too common out West here but you best be getting used to us."

Now it's my turn to frown. I study her more closely. She's at least in her early thirties, her pretty face is unlined but she has this authoritative air about her. Everything sounds like an accusation but one that's filled with a hint of doubt. Though she's trying hard to hide it, I can see she's as afraid of me as I am afraid of her.

I raise the infrared to her, slowly, as if she is a skittish cat, and show her the screen, flicking it on.

She looks at it and shakes her head, not getting it.

"It's infrared," I explain. "It picks up heat energy."

"Well my oh my," she says. "That's the dumbest thing I've ever heard. You trying to make a motion picture?"

"No m'am," I can't help but say. "Much less than that."

"And you what? You hunt ghosts?"

"It sounds ridiculous when you put it that way," I admit.

She snorts and turns around, heading back to the machines. "It sounds ridiculous anyway you put it, child."

"We've just been told the ghost of Parker Hayden is known to haunt this room."

She stops in mid-stride. Her whole body is tensed up. It makes me tense up too. I must have hit a nerve.

"Have you seen him?" I whisper, making sure the camera is running but not pointing it in her direction just yet. I don't want to scare her and just getting our dialog recorded would be more than enough for the show.

"Seen who?" she repeats slowly. She still doesn't turn around.

"Parker Hayden. The ship millionaire. He lost all of his money during the strike and then killed himself–"

"Don't you dare speak ill of him," she threatens in a low voice so raspy and ragged that it almost sounds demonic. "He would never kill himself."

I bite my lip, unsure of how to proceed. I have no idea what is going on but those hairs are standing up on the back of my neck again.

"Do you know who he was?" I ask carefully.

Finally, she turns around and looks at me with tear-filled eyes.

"He was...my friend."

I don't know what to make of that. "Pardon me?"

"He was...my lover. I haven't seen him for days, not since they threw him out."

Oh. Dear. God.

"He wouldn't have killed himself though," she continues, her voice warbling with emotion. A tear spills down her cheek, leaving a dark trail. "He has troubles but he wouldn't have done that. Not Parker. Not my Parker."

"Ummmm," is all I can say to that. I slowly raise the infrared camera and aim it at her.

"You're filming me now?"

Yes, I sure am, I think and look at the screen. My breath freezes in my throat. Through the infrared, I can see my own hand in front of me burning a deep red. The shape of the maid though is coming out a steely blue, like the blue I saw in the hotel room.

I look back at her. And I realize I'm talking to a ghost.

"I said, are you filming me? Answer me, child," she says, her voice angry. She wipes away a tear with a rough swipe of her hand.

"No," I say quickly and lower the camera. "Sorry, I... what did you say your name was?"

"I didn't. It's May," she answers. "I'd say I'm pleased to meet you Miss Perry Palomino, but I'm afraid I'm a victim of some terrible joke."

There's one thing I've learned about the dead: they don't like to learn they are dead. Things kind of go crazy when they do, like their entire existence is shattered and they go along with it. I mean, imagine you think you're alive and someone tells you you're dead. Then you start putting together all the pieces and BLAM! Your entire world is ripped apart. The very realization can make most ghosts simply disappear. The acceptance pushes them on into the afterlife, or whatever the next step is.

But for selfish reasons, I don't want to lose May. I don't want her to realize she's dead. Because while I've got her here, in this room, I can use her. I can use her to get to Parker.

"When was the last time you saw Parker?" I ask her innocently enough. I still keep the camera aimed at the floor.

"Five days ago," she says. "He said he'd come by the next day. I was here waiting. He never did. I reckoned...I don't know. I feared the worst. The very worst."

"Which was?"

"That he was dead, Miss Palomino. But not by his own hand. No, he that was murdered."

"By who?"

"The sharks. Who else?"

My face must have contorted into a look of pure confusion because she continues, her voice and demeanor more impassioned by the second.

"The sharks are the fellas who he owed money to. You just don't lose a boat without losing a few friends. These fellas meant business and I seen them threaten him more than a few times. Parker went and told the police but they do nothing. They don't have no control. Parker would tell me he was scared. So scared. He's a man who don't get scared, you hear that. So if he's scared, I reckon there's a reason for it. They are after his life."

The idea of Parker being murdered by men he owed money to is just as believable as suicide. I don't know what to believe but I choose to give the ghost the benefit of the doubt.

"Did Parker leave any proof, any records, that these men were after him?"

She closes her eyes for a second and it's then that I notice a strange transparency about her.

"There was his diary," she tells me. Her eyes open slowly. "It's his checkbook. But he would keep a log on the back of the checks he couldn't write anymore. Most of it doesn't make much sense to me...if I could talk to him, hear from him, he could tell you himself. I just need to talk to him. Can you find him for me? You said you knew the manager?"

"Yes...but I don't think it will make much difference."

"Why is that?"

"Do you know where he would have kept the checkbook?"

"On his person. Where else? What aren't you telling me? What are you really doing here?"

I look down at the screen and aim it at her. She glows a translucent blue. It's beautiful, for once, and not scary.

"What happened to Parker?" she goes on, her voice cracking over his name. I don't say anything but I meet her eye and I know, in one look, that she knows the truth. Maybe not that she's dead. But that he is.

Her face crumbles. She puts her hand to her head and stumbles backward.

Out of instinct, I go after her, my arms outstretched, hoping to reach her in time before she goes over.

I almost reach her when she smashes against the floor with a sickening thud. The world goes black. The lights go off and I find myself on my knees, my leggings ripping open on the cold hard floor.

"May?" I cry out and raise the camera, hoping to see her blue form through the darkness. I only read my own heat and no one else's.

I slowly get to my feet and try to flick on the flashlight with my own hand.

Cold fingers reach over my elbow in a stealthy grasp. I can feel the ice through my jacket.

I am yanked harshly to the side until I crash into a wheeled laundry bin and another hand grabs me by the face and pulls me over the side and into it.

All I can think about is the painful cold that comes from the grasp, as if permafrost is entering my veins and creating a sheet of ice on my face. And then I find myself face first in a laundry bin, smothered by a million towels and pulled deeper and deeper into them until I can't breathe and I can't scream and I can't move. I can only drown here.

The blackness behind my eyes grows darker somehow, as if the dark has a million different shades and nuances and I was only scratching the surface. It's a different kind of obsidian, one that signals the end, finality. I don't want to succumb to it, but all I can see is this blackness, and all I can feel are these hands that won't stop pulling me deeper, that won't let go, and my thoughts become less...and less...and less...

"Perry!"

I think I hear my name but it sounds too far away to be real. I think of May and wonder where she came from.

"Perry!"

My name again. It sounds familiar.

There is a rush of noise and light and commotion and I feel more hands grabbing me. Only these ones are warm and though they are strong, I can feel the care seeping through them.

I think of Dex. And remember where I am.

I put my hands at the bottom of the bin, and push myself off. As I do so, they come in contact with something beneath one of the towels. I'm afraid it's the remains of whoever was pulling me down before, but I still close my fingers around it as Dex yanks me out of the bin and into the harsh fluorescent light of the room.

I cough wildly, trying to find my breath as Dex keeps his hands on either side of my shoulders, steadying me. As the air hits my lungs and my wincing subsides, I notice Pam standing beside the door, a key in hand, her face in a look of absolute terror.

"Perry," Dex says. "Perry look at me."

I manage to look at him. His dark eyes are searching mine relentlessly, his brow furrowed, his stance tense.

"Are you OK?" he asks.

I nod, feeling relieved and embarrassed all at the same time.

"Was I sticking out of the laundry bin?" I ask with trepidation.

He nods and I see a hint of a smile tug at the corner of

his mouth. It would have been a comical sight, my giant ass in the air and all.

"I leave you alone for five seconds..." His tone is light but he knows there is more to the story. And that I'll fill him in on it later.

"What's in your hands?" Pam asks, looking at them with curiosity.

I glance down and see I am holding a rectangular cover of well-worn leather. I open it carefully and see what I thought I would see. A checkbook filled with writing. The possible proof that Parker Hayden was murdered and not a victim of suicide.

I walk over to Pam and place the item in her hands. She looks up at me surprised and confused.

"You may want to run this by a historian. Or even the police," I say. "There's a chance that Parker Hayden didn't commit suicide after all. It could be a cold case file. A very cold case."

I feel extremely cheesy as I tell Pam that. No surprise, Dex says, "Wow, I leave you for one minute and suddenly you're CSI: Portland."

I give him a tired smile. I'm ready to go home.

A FEW DAYS PASS WHEN I GET A CALL FROM DEX. We're not at the point where we call each other just to talk, but every contact I have with him is still important and I still get stupid butterflies every time I see his name pop up on the call display. This time, he's calling to talk about our episode at The Benson.

"How's it all looking?" I ask as I sit on my bed, listening to my younger sister Ada argue with my dad downstairs.

"Oh it's looking fucking fantastic, kiddo," Dex says, his voice coming in low and smooth over the line. "I just want to hug you for keeping that camera rolling while May was talking. I'll have to run it over some other footage and do that little subtitle thing underneath but it really helps our case, especially when you get that blue shit on screen. That really is something."

"Best show ever?" I ask, amused at his praise.

"Well," he says slowly, "it probably would have helped had I been around but you did OK on your own."

"I'll take that as a compliment."

"There's something else, too, you should take as a compliment."

My eyes perk up and I sit up a bit straighter, putting down my Spin magazine. "What's that?"

"Pam just called me. She said she handed over the checkbook to the police who are having a division look into it or something. Anyway, the point is ever since our visit, all the haunting in the hotel has stopped."

"What do you mean, all hauntings?"

"Well she says she usually gets some sort of feedback each day. Since our shoot, there hasn't been any. I don't know what that means but she seems to think that whatever you did down in that laundry room...well, I guess you cleared the place."

"So I'm an exorcist now?"

"Don't flatter yourself, kiddo. You're miles away from being Father Merrin and for all we know the haunting could start up again. I'm just saying...next time you feel like being hard on yourself because we aren't making a difference and there's no point to any of this...I dunno. Don't. Because you did good here. You did good."

I let Dex ramble on a bit more to please my ego and

then we hang up. Like the other times before, I still don't know what to make of my ghost hunting. I don't know how I got roped into doing the show, how I ended up being a magnet for the supernatural and what on earth it has in store for me. The only thing I do know is that it's dangerous and I'm compelled to keep doing it.

But I also know that even though someone is dead, is doesn't mean they're beyond help. And for every ten ghosts that try and kill me, if I end up saving one of them, it might be worth it after all.

Though you may want to remind me of that, next time I'm locked in a coffin or something.

Continue the ghost-hunting adventures of Perry and Dex by reading:

Dead Sky Morning – Experiment in Terror #3

"With the Experiment in Terror show finding some success, amateur ghost hunters Perry Palomino and Dex Foray embark on their most terrifying investigation yet. A tiny, fog-shrouded island in the rough strait between British Columbia and Washington State has held a dark secret for decades: It was a former leper colony where over forty souls were left to rot, die and bury each other. Now a functioning campground, Perry and Dex spend an isolated weekend there to investigate potential hauntings but as the duo quickly find out, there is more to fear on D'Arcy Island than just ghosts. The island quickly pits partner against partner, spiraling the pair into madness that serves to destroy their sanity, their relationship and their very lives."

CHAPTER ONE

My mind reeled awake like the slow wind of undeveloped film. Everything was black. Very black. A shade of coal darker than anything behind closed eyes. But my eyes weren't closed at all. They were open and squinting against a light mist that burned them like salt.

Where was I?

I couldn't bring my mind around fast enough to remember anything concrete. But there were thoughtless flashes. The reel in my head spun wildly, more shady images skittering past the spokes. There was a forest. I was running. I was hunted down by hounds. Or humans on four legs. Their grotesque figures flickered in the woods like a waning pilot light.

Then nothing.

"My watery grave." The phrase floated around in my head.

I lay still. I was on my back, on top of something awkward and bony. I told my limbs to move but nothing happened. I concentrated, desperately finding some light my retinas could latch on to, to give some meaning to where I was and what was happening to me.

There were sounds, suddenly, like ear plugs were plucked out of my head. I heard muffled cries, like someone was yelling from far away and the sloshing sounds of water encompassing the space around me. I had the distinct feeling that I was floating as my inner ear rolled and swayed inside my heavy head.

All my senses were coming to me now. I could smell seawater and a putrid, decaying odor, like rotted fruit and mold. I felt dampness at my back and, bit by bit, the sensation that my hands were emerged in ice cold water.

I tried to move my arms again and this time they responded sluggishly. They had been in water all this time even though the rest of me was dry. I moved them out to the sides and they struck barriers with a force I barely felt through my numbed skin. The sound of the impact echoed around me. It told me I was in some sort of box or...or...

Panic swept through me. I moved again, feeling like I was balanced precipitously on top of something very peculiar. Whatever it was, it was smaller than the length of my body and I noticed my legs had dropped off below at an angle. I kicked them up. A spray of ice water fell up on top of my shins and my waterlogged boots thunked against something solid.

I felt all around me, wildly placing my hands and feet on whichever surface they could reach. I was in a box after all. The space above my head was only about half a foot before a damp wooden ceiling cut me off from the rest of the world.

I tried to catch my breath but the fright inside my chest was overpowering it. I was trapped, trapped in a box. A mime's worst nightmare.

Not only that, but a box that was filling with water. I felt the liquid fingers crawling up my legs and arms and saturating my back.

I started writhing and fighting. I couldn't keep it together any longer. I was in a box and I was going to drown in here.

I started pounding my hands against the top, hoping to break through. They were tired and without much feeling. I felt a gush of warmth flowing from them. It was my blood. It seeped freely from my tender knuckles and from the wounds at my both my wrists. I didn't care. I had to get out. If I didn't, I would die.

The water came in faster now and it wasn't long before I was slightly buoyant, rising above whatever was below me. In seconds it would come over the tops of my pants. My pants, where my front pocket felt tighter than usual.

I quickly slipped my hand into the pocket on a hunch. There was the lighter in there.

I pulled it out and started to flicker it. My fingers were cold and clumsy and I almost dropped it but after a few awkward attempts, the flame came alive, the spark catching hold. I held it up and away from me. The weak, orange light illuminated the space around me.

I was right. I was in a box.

It wasn't just a box though. No it wasn't. I knew what it was.

My watery grave.

I swallowed hard, feeling my world jar wildly with the incoming waves. I was in a coffin, set adrift in the sea.

"Your ship has come in." A man's voice echoed inside my head.

Amidst all the commotion, among all the confusion over what had happened – I knew where I was and why I was here. I wished I was alone. But I knew that wasn't true either. I knew that awkward, protruding, lumpy shape beneath me spared me of that luxury.

My left hand slipped into the water, gingerly feeling the bottom of the casket. Maybe the only way out was through the bottom. I was careful now to avoid what was directly beneath me.

The water was up to my chest now. I was running out of time and fast.

I placed my hand on the bottom and tried to stabilize one part of me while I planned to kick out with my legs, hoping that the splintery walls would give way.

Tiny, slimy fingers made their way around my submerged wrist.

I screamed but it escaped through my lips like a word-less gasp. The fingers tightened like a tiny clamp and held my wrist down, drowning it.

Something shot out from the water beside me and knocked the lighter out of my hands, enveloping the casket in darkness again. My arm was seized by another miniature grasp. It yanked me down into the water.

I tried to move, to yell, to fight, but the water's chill had seized me like poison. I was being held down; the water was rising and almost to my face.

Something moved beneath my head. It came up close to my submerged ear. Someone whispered into it.

The voice was distorted and muffled underwater. But it was unmistakable.

"Mother!" it cried out, cold child lips brushing my earlobe.

I opened my mouth to scream again but only found water. I took it in instead of air and let the liquid saturate the life out of me.

"Mother" it said again and again until we were floating together and the world closed its eyes.

"Excuse me?" a strange voice said from behind me.

I took my change from the coffee shop barista, giving her a short smile in the process, and carefully turned around to see who was talking. It sounded more like a hesitant question and not a plea to get by.

A pleasant heavy–set man in a windbreaker, holding a coffee and pastry, was behind me off to the side of the line. He had that look in his squidgy eyes that said he recognized me. But for the life of me, I had no idea who he was.

I gave him an even shorter smile than the one I had imparted seconds earlier. I don't get picked up all that often but it happened enough that it made me leery anytime some strange man attempted to talk to me.

"Uh huh?" I said, trying to be polite but still seem uninterested.

His cheeks puffed up when he saw my face more clearly. He let out a little guffah that stood out against the coffee shop's irritating music.

"You're the ghost lady," he said, smiling, pointing at me with his pastry bag.

I frowned. Was I the ghost lady?

He took a step closer to me and jabbed the pastry in the

air again, pink frosting falling off it and snowing onto the tiles below.

"You're the one on the internet," he exclaimed, just a bit too loud for comfort. I looked around awkwardly, feeling strangely embarrassed at what was happening. A girl in line was looking at me, obviously not impressed given her once–over, but no one else was paying attention. Typical hipsters.

I looked back at him and smiled again, despite the burning, tight sensation on my own cheeks.

"Oh. So you've seen *Experiment in Terror?*" I asked.

"Yes, of course," he said, chuckling to himself, the jowls in his throat waving back and forth. "I just stumbled upon it a few weeks ago. I love it. It's very *Blair Witch Project*. You know, it's real. We all know the *Blair Witch Project* wasn't real, but you know, this seems real. It is real, right?"

"Yeah, it's real," I said slowly, aware that every time I admitted the show was real it made either a believer or a disbeliever out of someone.

"I could tell. I knew that was real fear in your eyes. Sorry, it's Perry. Perry Palomino, right?"

"That's me," I said, feeling more comfortable with the situation. He was just a fan of the show. A fan of my show. A fan of me. My first fan!

"Well, I'll let you get your coffee," he said as he aimed the pastry over at the counter, where a barista was placing my latte down haphazardly, foamy milk spilling down the sides of the cup and seeping into the cardboard sleeve. "Keep up the good work!"

And just like that, he spun around and shuffled out of the coffee shop, munching away on his confection as he rounded the corner.

I wiped off the sides of the latte with a napkin and shook my head. Not so much about the sloppy coffee presentation but the fact that someone not only liked what I was doing, but had actually recognized me enough to stop and say hello. It was unnerving and exciting at the same time.

So much had changed over the last few weeks. The trip I took to the town of Red Fox in New Mexico had done a number on me. Having nearly died at the hands of two bitter and deranged ranchers/lovers turned skinwalkers, it really made me rethink my current situation. Mainly, did I want to be involved in hosting a "shitty" internet show about the supernatural when our very subject possessed the ability to not only hurt us, but kill us? I mean, despite my run–ins with Ol' Roddy at my Uncle Al's lighthouse, the possibility of death hadn't really been in the job description.

That's all I was able to think about on the flight home from Albuquerque. Dex had gone on his merry way back to Seattle and I was alone with only my thoughts and my iPod to accompany me on the way to Portland. Too much had happened on that weekend, aside from the fact that we were exposed to a type of danger that most people would never be in. My beliefs in what was possible in this world, in my reality, were ripped to shreds. My partner, who I still barely knew, had become the closest person to me (in more ways than one). And the show began to resemble nothing more than a vain attempt at notoriety through the most amateur of all mediums. After all, who wasn't famous on the internet these days?

On top of that, there was the fact that I was living a lie to my parents, pretending I had a job when in fact I had been fired from the advertising agency just before.

But within a matter of days of my return, when the nightmares of zombie coyotes and shape–shifting bears began to fade, everything seemed to right itself. It's almost as if it was my destiny to keep going, to keep our web show *Experiment in Terror* alive, and to keep Dex Foray in my life.

Dex sent me over the footage of what we managed to capture in Red Fox, and the results blew me away. So much so that I had to watch it with my younger sister Ada; otherwise I would have probably shit myself. Though not everything was captured on film, the fact is, everything really happened and it wasn't hard for me to mentally fill in the missing pieces we collected on digital film. Even Ada was scared by the whole ordeal. She had already known the whole story but seeing parts of it come alive must have throttled her.

It was hard to know what the public was going to do with the whole thing so I did the best I could and wrote up everything on the blog that would accompany the footage. I changed some people's names to protect the innocent (Dex had actually blurred out the face of Will Lancaster, the man who was tormented by the skinwalkers – I think that was a guilty reaction on his part) but I told the story exactly as it happened. I knew that a lot of people (probably 80% of viewers) wouldn't believe a word of it but it was truth, and to quote Fox Mulder, the truth was out there.

Luckily, whether people accepted the truth or not, *Experiment in Terror* got its proper (i.e. not a demo) debut on the Shownet website that following Sunday.

It was...amazing. OK, I know what you're thinking; of course, it was amazing because I was in it. No, not at all. In fact, I was barely in it (which I kind of liked – still not used to this whole "on camera" thing yet). But there was no denying that the show actually looked great. In combination with my blog and with the score Dex somehow whipped up in a week, "Red Fox" actually worked.

We had a show. Even my parents looked a tad more impressed about it (and they are the show's toughest critics). Dex would send me text messages throughout the week keeping me informed on hits to the website and if people were linking to it. That one episode was becoming a bit of a phenomenon, just as my original footage of my adventures in my uncle's lighthouse had been. Well, a small phenomenon, but that still surpassed any of the doubts I had earlier about the future of the show and my involvement in it.

The next step to ensure our success continued was for me to make Twitter and Facebook accounts for the show and manage them. I knew enough from my marketing programs at the university that we had to promote as much as possible. And since Dex was busy being a composer, a filmmaker, editor, and trying to arrange future filming opportunities, that all fell into my hands.

It had been a lot of fun, actually, even though all the "tweeting" became a bit of a crutch when I should have been applying for jobs. Then came Dex's brilliant idea to open the blog to comments. By the way, I say brilliant in the most sarcastic way. Opening the blog comments did increase a sort of communal feel on Shownet, and maybe attracted more attention overall, but unfortunately a lot of the comments were rather negative.

At first it was just people like ALEX64 saying things like, "This show is crap, what bullshit" and that sort of stuff, which is to be expected. I couldn't say I wouldn't want to say the same thing. Without a ghost (or whatever) coming up to you and slapping you in your own face, it was a hard thing to fathom and even now I had a hard time coming to terms with what happened. Honestly, it was easier to just pretend it was all a figment of your imagination than to accept that the world, as most people know it, is just an illusion, and predatory, evil, things really do lurk in the shadows. Lately, though, the comments were getting a bit personal.

Two weeks ago, Dex had come to Portland so we could do some filming. We ended up actually filming two different places that weekend – Portland has no shortage of haunted tales. The first place we hit up was The Benson Hotel, which always had a scary reputation. It's actually a really nice hotel with a spiffy doorman outside and everything, and most people have a very pleasant and lovely stay. Still, there was always someone, at least once a week, complaining to management about seeing a strange lady roaming the hallways and the grand staircase, or weird sounds and noises, or random stuff going missing. A lot of staff workers acknowledged that weird things did happen, but no one seemed very bothered by it, evidenced by a local "Ghost Walk" tour that poked around every weekend.

So when we showed up at the hotel, they didn't bat an eye. They said that we could roam freely in the hotel and poke around (without poking around in people's hotel rooms, of course).

We didn't really see anything too out of the ordinary. I was still scared out of my wits, as usual. It didn't seem to matter if I was getting attacked by animals in the fathomless New Mexico desert or if I'd seen a ghostly apparition in the elevator of a crowded hotel; I still got scared. But there was nothing wanting to kill us (a nice change) or anything really sending our minds packing. Just a load of things that "could be," which always becomes "is" in my own overworked mind. And thanks to Dex's clever work and bit of luck, we were able to convey the same thing on film. We caught a lot of weird floating orbs of light, and picked up weird heat shapes on the infrared camera.

Same thing happened the next day when we spent the entire night at a haunted pizza joint that used to house a brothel. Apparently the madam had been found at the bottom of the old elevator shaft with her neck broken; the verdict was murder. We often heard people walking around in the upper dining area (when we knew no one was up there) and we managed to get that on film. And the basement, the basement was something else. Hot and cold spots everywhere, more weird orbs and an incredibly creepy feeling at every turn. Even Dex, who is normally quite composed when he's filming, said he was happy to get out of there.

We had aimed to film something every weekend but as our series was just getting off the ground, and I had to keep up the illusion that I was still working for most of the week, that wasn't feasible. Luckily, filming both the hotel and the pizza parlor on one weekend allowed us to get two episodes out of it.

I'm getting a bit off track. Anyway, the hotel episode "The Benson" just aired and to as much applause as the "Red Fox" episode did. Unfortunately, that also meant the comments were coming in as well, and this time they were meaner. More personal, as I said. Someone "Anonymous" (aren't they always?) had started attacking me and the way I looked. Saying I was too fat to be on camera, that I was ugly, that I looked stupid and sounded stupid. You get the idea.

The worst part of it all was that I believed it. This anonymous coward was just reinstating everything I felt about myself already. I had always felt like I was too heavy to be on camera. I always felt ugly and I knew for sure I sounded stupid.

I know I should just shrug it all off. I know that the internet is a terrible place that attracts terrible people who wouldn't have the balls to say anything if they had to put a face to their name. But it was getting harder each day. Yes, some people said some nice things in defense of me (I wasn't fat, I had a pretty face, I sounded knowledgeable) but it was only the negative things I believed.

I wanted to tell Dex that perhaps we should switch off the comment section, or run it with a moderator, but I couldn't figure out how to bring it up without sounding totally insecure. Although I had been in daily texting contact with Dex, and sometimes it wasn't even work–related, I wasn't in that place where I could just tell him how I felt.

Back in New Mexico, after spending almost every waking (and sleeping...but just sleeping) moment with him, I had felt so connected to him. I know it makes me sound like some blathering girl, but I honestly felt like he and I were on the same page. We were finally communicating.

But since we got back, I only saw him for that weekend in Portland. Because it was my hometown, I just stayed at home and he got a cheap motel by the airport. I saw him when we did our filmmaking, and there were a few times I thought maybe something was going to happen (what, I don't know) but then he would go back to his motel and I would go back to my parents' house. All the intimacy I had felt in Red Fox was gone.

And the contact we had now was just in text messages and emails. I can't lie and pretend that I didn't get kind of giddy and stupidly smiley every time a message from him came in, even if it said something as simple as "liked what you wrote" or "I hate the new Muse album." But that was the extent of our "relationship" at the moment. It was like the kiss never happened.

Yeah. The kiss. It weighed on my mind. It's what my thoughts turned to whenever they drifted away for a few seconds. It's the feelings that were stirred up when the wind on the street caught my face just right, or when a certain song came on shuffle. Dex had kissed me, as we were perched up in a swaying pine tree, as we were certain we would meet our deaths below.

It seemed appropriate at the time. I thought I was going to die and I know he did too. But it couldn't have been just that, could it? Couldn't it have meant more, couldn't it have been something he had always wanted to do? I know it was something more to me. I'd been wanting to lay my lips on him ever since we first met.

There was Jennifer though, Dex's mega–babe girlfriend. The tiny, pathetic voice in my head, the one that so hopelessly wished that maybe they'd be through after our trip, was stifled. They hadn't broken up. The kiss meant nothing in the end. Dex was back with Jenn and back to his zany self.

Well, sorta. He had been off his medication in New Mexico (accidently) and though he had a few rough patches he was sort of normal, for lack of a better word, by the time we parted ways. Yet when I saw him again he seemed off. Bored, in a way. The playful banter we had shared was subdued and the bright, zealous light that sparked from his eyes had dimmed. He was obviously back on his medication again, or perhaps some new one, but whatever "illness" it was keeping at bay was also keeping the real Dex at bay as well. I didn't think it was a fair tradeoff. Yes, Dex was manic and often behaved like a wind–up toy but that was who he was. The last night in Red Fox I had told him I hoped he would always feel alive. I think my words fell on deaf ears.

But I was probably overthinking and overanalyzing everything as I always did. I wouldn't be surprised if I thought he'd changed just because of the circumstances. I mean, they *had* changed. I think I just had to accept that our relationship was going to change each time we were together. We were partners, we kept in touch and when we were together, we were at the mercy of something else. When we weren't, he went back to Jennifer and I went back to awaiting his texts like a naïve schoolgirl.

That dilemma aside, which was really just a need to keep my wandering feelings in check, everything really had fallen in place. Though last week's trip was canceled due to bad weather, we were supposed to embark on a trip to a haunted old leper colony in British Columbia, Canada, on the weekend. Our next episode, the pizza parlor one, would air when we were gone. And my 23rd birthday was the next week.

Everything had fallen into place, except the whole job thing. I was still looking, every day, for someplace to hire me, still lying daily to my parents about having a career. In fact, my 4 p.m. coffee ritual in the lobby of Portland's Ace Hotel signaled the end of my job search day. Another empty day of holing up in various internet cafes, writing worthless cover letters that would never be read and applying for jobs that companies wouldn't give more than a glance to.

I sighed and poured a packet of sugar–free sweetener in my coffee, watching the chemicals dissolve in the hot frothy liquid. It was frustrating, to say the least, having to spend so much effort in trying to get a job. It was almost like a job itself, but of course it didn't pay.

But as long as my parents didn't find out about it, I was going to be OK. Although, it was annoying and extremely stressful to keep on lying to them. So much so that I barely had an appetite (actually that boded quite well in one way; I'd lost a few pounds – take that, Anonymous!) and the guilt I had was tearing me up inside at night, clouding my dreams and filling me with shame when I was the most vulnerable. I had no choice but to deal with it though, and keep filling out stupid applications and whore my resume around town.

At least that guy had recognized me and looked pleased with himself for doing so. He was a fan of the show. That little encounter, as panicky as it made me feel, did a lot to raise my spirits.

I wanted to text Dex and tell him what happened. He'd probably get a kick out of it.

I brought out my phone but noticed I already had a text message. Before I got a chance to get excited, I noticed it was from Ada, not Dex.

–DO NOT COME HOME TODAY– it said. All caps, too.

A wave of nausea swept over me. I was simultaneously disturbed and puzzled.

I put the coffee back down on the condiments counter and texted her back.

–What do you mean?–

I sent it and decided to plunk myself at a table that was miraculously empty at this caffeine rush hour. Normally the 4 p.m. coffee break meant I took my latte back to my motorbike, Put–Put, which was parked a few blocks away, and finished it on the walk there. But if my sister was telling me not to come home, I wasn't in a huge rush.

I sat around for five minutes, fingers nervously picking at the rubber iPhone cover. Ada hadn't texted back.

What did it mean, don't come home? I looked back at my calls and texts from the day. There was a text from Dex earlier saying that the weather for the weekend looked like it was cooperating and there was a missed call from my father. I had called him back, though, and no one answered. I didn't think it was a big deal. He often called to ask me stupid questions (you know, "what's the name of that actor in that cop show, yadda yadda"), whereas my mother would call to make sure I was "fine."

Other than that, there were no clues, and Ada wasn't responding. I looked at the time the message was sent: A half hour ago. I keep my phone on silent but normally check it once an hour to see what had gone through. Though to be honest, I was checking it more and more lately in case someone had responded to one of my tweets, or Facebook postings, or if someone else had said something nasty on the blog.

Ada probably meant to send the text to someone else (it had happened before) or maybe she had a boy over or something. I didn't know, but what I did know was that I wasn't going to keep sitting in the coffee shop and pretending to drink my latte, which I had already downed.

I shrugged off the uneasy feeling, tossed the coffee in the trash and stepped out into the street. It was a mild pre–winter Wednesday in early November, less than a week before my birthday. I hated thinking about it. I had been fine with turning 22, but turning 23 took on a whole new meaning for me. It was closer to 25 than anything else and 25 had always been the age I figured I'd have my shit together.

That said, some stranger had just complimented me on my TV show (OK, fine, "internet" show) and that wasn't exactly something I had planned on achieving before I turned 25. Maybe this was just a sign of good things to come, all the things that I needed to acquire before I turned 25: A boyfriend, a condo in the city all my own and a job that showed people what I was really made of. Or maybe it would just help the last part. Either way, it wasn't anything to sneeze at.

That thought made me feel more confident as I walked over to the meter where I had parked Put–Put, and piloted him through the cold winds that ruffled my back and propelled me home.

CHAPTER TWO

I pulled Put–Put into my parents' driveway, amazed at how dark it was already. The clocks had gone back last week and I still hadn't adjusted to the perpetual gloominess. I hated knowing it would be a long time before the sun was bright and the days were long.

I eyed the house warily. The lights were on. The warm contrast against the darkness would have normally made me feel all cozy inside, but it made me feel strangely anxious instead, like the house was alive and waiting for me. I wasn't sure what that meant but I knew I probably had to trust my instincts. They were right most of the time.

I walked over to the front door, slowly fishing out my key. I paused on the bottom step. A strange wave of energy radiated towards me from the closed door. My anxious feeling intensified. I looked around me, wondering what it could be. A movement at my bedroom window on the second floor caught my eye.

It was Ada. Her small frame was barely visible against

my room, which was lit only by my desk lamp. She was waving at me frantically, making the shooing motion.

I was about to step back and holler at her, hoping she would open the window and explain what was going on, when the front door flew open. My father was on the other side.

"Are you going to come inside?" he bellowed.

This was not the normal greeting from my father. Though it was hard to see his face since he was backlit by the foyer, I could tell he was scowling. Few things strike fear in my heart quite like my father does when he's angry. Ghosts and skinwalkers were one thing, but my dad was something else. Something I understood. Our tempers were unfortunately very similar.

I swallowed hard. "I was just looking for my keys."

He glanced down at the keys visible in my hand and walked back in the house. I didn't want to follow him but I had no choice.

I walked inside and closed the door gently behind me. He had disappeared. I shook off my boots, placing them neatly in the hall closet instead of leaving them lying on the floor like I usually did, and creeped forward down the hall-way, hoping that I could get to the stairs and the safety of my room before anything happened.

"Perry?" I heard my mother call out from the living room.

I turned to my left and saw her and my father sitting on separate armchairs. They looked like a job–interviewing panel. In the light of the room, my dad was indeed scowling. He was sucking in his cheeks, something he did when he was keeping the verbal volcano on lockdown. Underneath his glasses, his eyes explored my mother's face and avoided my own.

My mother looked rather blank except for the lines of worry that always wiggled on her forehead. I didn't like this situation at all.

I heard a noise behind me and turned to see Ada standing awkwardly on the staircase, staring at me frightfully. Her eyes were red like she had been crying and her makeup was more smudged than normal, which said a lot.

"Go back to your room, Ada," my dad said forcefully without looking at her.

Ada's eyes met with mine and I could almost hear her saying, 'I told you to not come home' in my head. Then she ran up the stairs and I was left feeling very alone and very scared.

"I called you today, Perry," my father said thickly.

"Uh, I know. I called you back but no one answered."

"I wanted to know if you wanted to go out for lunch with me since I was heading into the city."

"Oh. Sorry," I stammered. My heart began to thump louder. This was not just about missing a lunch with my dad. I knew deep down inside what this was all about.

"So, I decided to surprise you and stop by your office," he said, his eyes focusing on me like a laser beam.

My heart must have stopped. It felt like it fell out from my chest and onto the floor, along with my lungs and nerves. It's exactly what I was afraid of. He knew. They knew. I was done for.

I couldn't say anything. What was there to say? The room swayed.

He continued, "Do you know what I found when I got to your office? I saw a strange receptionist. And when I asked if I could speak with you, I was told that you no longer worked for the company. Naturally, I got a little upset."

Oh God. I could just see my father blowing a gasket in the middle of my old work, disturbing the stuffy advertising suits just as I had done on more than a few occasions.

"And then your boss – sorry, your ex–boss – came out and explained to me what happened. She had told me they had to let you go. You took your promotion and then demanded you be allowed to work part–time."

My father continued on, trying very hard to keep his voice down and in control. I stopped listening. His voice wavered in and out of my ears without sinking past the first barrier. I looked at my mother but was unable to read her face. I knew she was disappointed in me too and that was probably an understatement.

"Are you listening to me?" my dad shouted, rising up out of his chair, his stocky body hovering over me. I had no choice but to listen. "Do you know how, how *fucking* humiliating it was to discover you had been fired?"

I winced and took a step backward. My dad was religious and never, ever swore. I couldn't remember the last time I had seen him that angry. Maybe back in high school when I was involved in that "accident."

I felt tears pricking the back of my eyes and a building feeling of hate and frustration flowing up through my throat. I was either going to vomit or yell back at him. The former would be a million times more preferable.

"We trusted you! You lied to us. For weeks!" he screamed, spittle flying off his lips and into my face.

"I had to!" I yelled back, unable to keep it down. "You wouldn't have understood at all!"

"Don't raise your voice at me!" he yelled even louder.

I bit my lip hard, hard enough so that I tasted the bitter salt of blood and clenched my fists until I felt all the energy getting choked in them.

"All of this for some stupid show. A show based on lies! A show that makes you look like a total idiot. Useless, meaningless and stupid."

The dam burst. Tears spilled out of my eyes, my fingers uncurled and picked up the nearest object, a lamp, and gripped it in my hands, ready to throw it across the room.

"Don't you fucking call me stupid!" I screamed. The scream came up like an overpowering wave of anger, like it was a cloud of pure hatred rising out of my body. My world blurred for a split second as the feelings drowned me.

Then...

All the paintings on the wall shook violently and fell to the ground in a simultaneous smash.

I froze. So did my father. I saw a flicker of fear behind his eyes. My mother covered her face in her hands and whimpered, "Not again" to herself.

I was panting heavily, trying to catch my breath as the fuzzy threads of unconsciousness began to fade in the corner of my mind. The living room carpet was bordered with glass fragments. Had my scream brought them down off their hooks? Was that possible?

My dad looked around him, dumbfounded, and back at me. He opened his mouth to say something but then thought better of it. He walked over to my mother and patted her on the back. She was crying softly.

"You see what you did. You're scaring your mother again," he said. His voice had quieted but the accusatory tone was still there.

I took in a deep breath and carefully placed the lamp back on the table. My emotions were coming back around. I didn't need to break the lamp in order to prove my point.

"I'm sorry," I said feebly. "I should have told you I got

fired but I didn't want you to know. I was afraid you'd make me quit the show."

"Damn right you're going to quit the show," my dad said.

The urge to explode was rising again. I eyed the lamp.

"Perry, please don't start this," my mom whispered through her hands. I paused. She looked up at me, her eyes pleading. Not from concern but from fright. She was afraid of me.

I wanted to ask what she meant by "this" but I didn't. That seemed like a path I didn't need to go down at the moment.

"I'm not quitting," I managed to squeak out. There was no way that was happening. It wasn't an option. They should have known that.

"Perry," my father warned.

"No. No, I am not quitting. This job is all I have!" The panic in my voice was unmistakable.

He laughed. It was bitter, angry. "It's not a job. I have a job, Perry."

"It pays. I am making money. I signed a contract to be employed by ShowNet. So it is a job." I was losing my patience and afraid I was losing the war.

"I am not discussing this with you further. As long as you live in this house, you will not be doing that show."

"Oh yeah? Well, try and stop me," I said, crossing my arms, surprised at my own stubbornness and nerve.

He looked surprised too. He sat back down in his armchair with a heavy sigh and pinched the bridge of his nose.

My mother spoke up gently, "Perry, we're more concerned with the fact that you lied to us. I didn't think you would lie like that anymore."

"I said I was sorry," I mumbled but kept my stance. "And I am sorry. I feel terrible about it. I haven't been able to sleep, I haven't been able to eat. And I'm not lazing around doing nothing, I'm out every day looking for jobs. It's just hard. No one is hiring."

"This wouldn't be a problem if you hadn't messed everything up," dad said. "You had a chance for a great career and you threw it away. I mean, you actually had it in your hands, Perry. We were so proud of you. Why did you have to ruin it? Why do you have to make problems for yourself? You need to just...grow up."

The tears were coming again. Not from anger or frustration but because I truly did feel terrible. I hated lying to them and even more than that, I hated the fact that they thought less of me.

The tears spilled down my cheeks but I tried to hold it together.

"I'm so sorry," I said again, feeling utterly, destructively helpless.

"Just...go, Perry. Your mother and I have a lot to talk about," my father said, turning his attention away from me. It was like he couldn't even look in my direction anymore.

I sniffled, wiping my tears on my coat jacket and took off up the stairs, my vision blurring. I almost tripped on the last step but suddenly Ada was beside me and had me by the arm. We didn't say anything to each other; she just took me down the hall to her room and led me inside. I stumbled through my tears and flopped onto her bed.

I spent a few minutes heaving into the down comforter, my sobs choking my breath. Ada patted me on the back and I was thankful for the rare affection from my little sister.

"Parents just don't understand," I said into the blanket, my voice muffled.

"What?" she asked.

I rolled over and gave her a weak smile. "Will Smith was onto something."

She still looked puzzled at my old school rap reference. "Whatever. I'm sorry they found out."

"Did they figure out you knew?"

She nodded. No wonder it looked like she had been crying. They laid into her for lying for me, for trying to save my ass. I felt very guilty for bringing her into my mess, for having to cover up my lies. I told her that.

"It's OK," she said licking her finger and wiping away her mascara smudges on her cheeks. "They were mad, though. Dad said some pretty mean stuff."

"I bet Mom wasn't an angel either," I scoffed.

She tilted her head. "Actually...Mom was standing up for you."

I sat up a bit straighter. "Really?"

My mom and I weren't exactly close. We never had been. That feeling that I had earlier, that she was afraid of me...it didn't exactly come from nowhere. I always felt my mom treated me with kid gloves, more for her own concern than mine.

"Yeah. She thought maybe this would lead you to something better down the road. The show. Not the whole fake job thing. She even told Dad it wasn't that big of a deal if you didn't have a job at the moment since you were living at home anyway."

That didn't sound like my mom at all.

"You're sure?"

She shrugged and got off the bed. She peered in the mirror. "I don't know, it's just what she said. Then Dad ended up yelling at her. You know, the usual stupid shit.

And I ran away while I could. And that's why I told your stupid ass not to come home."

Well, would it have killed you to text a little more information? I thought, but didn't say anything. She had done enough for me already.

She glanced at me. "So what are you going to do now? What are you going to say to Dex?"

Dex. Oh shit. For the first time in awhile, I had completely forgotten about him.

"You going to call him?" She came over to the bed and sat beside me.

"I can't deal with that now," I said, though I knew I would have to tell him something. I was supposed to meet him in Seattle on Friday.

It was just too much. My head began to spin wildly and I fell back into the covers, closing my eyes, wanting to shut everything out.

"Want me to text him?" she asked.

I sighed. "Could you?"

She reached into my coat pocket and pulled my phone out. "There's only one Dex in your contacts, right?"

I nodded.

"OK, well what do you want me to write? Sorry dude, I have to bail. Forever..." She trailed off dramatically.

"Oh, give it to me," I said impatiently, and snatched it from her hands. If I had to think about what to say, I might as well write it myself.

I typed the first thing that came to my head.

– Bad news. My parents are forbidding me to do the show. I'm so sorry. I'll try and talk them out of it but no promises. I am so sorry. –

I hesitated before pressing Send. It felt like a cop–out.

But I did press it and threw the phone away from me. I covered my eyes with my hands.

"Ugh."

I waited a few seconds before I nervously eyed it. It was on silent after all.

Ada followed my gaze and peered at the phone.

"Nothing yet," she said. She looked back at me, "What are you more upset about? Losing the show or losing Dex?"

The question startled me. It was oddly accurate. "Who are you, my shrink now?"

"Well, since the old shrink quit, I –" she started with a smirk.

"Shut up," I cut her off.

"Hey," she smacked my leg. "You owe me, stupid head."

"I know." I just wanted to avoid the question. Finally I said, "It's both."

That was the truth. I was terrified of losing the show because it's all I had going for me. It's what kept me going, kept my confidence, kept a strange sense of importance and destiny in my soul. It's like I was meant to do this (do something) after years of searching blindly for anything that made me feel like I was as good enough as anyone else, or hell, even better, and I didn't want to let it go.

And Dex. I couldn't let Dex go. It was no secret I was in love with him, no matter how hard I tried to push my feelings down or rationalize it in some logical way. I just loved the guy. I know I didn't know him that well – but I loved what I did know. And what I didn't know drove me crazy like some book that you can't stop reading, just to see how it ends, just to see if your hunches were right. The thought of losing him, even as just his dorky little partner, pained me. Literally. The more I thought about it, the more my heart seized up in sharp little spasms. I put my hand on my chest in an effort to soothe it.

There was pity in Ada's big blue eyes. She knew. I didn't have to say anything. Silence enveloped us both as I got lost in my own thoughts, and she in hers.

"Things will work out," she eventually said.

I really wanted to believe that. "Must be nice to be young and optimistic."

"You're young too."

"Well, I'm not 15-years old anymore. When I was 15, I thought I was invincible. And don't say anything about how I was all fucked up back then; it's not part of my point."

She kept her snide remarks to herself and looked over at the phone. An apprehensive wave flashed across her brow. I knew the text had come through.

She handed it to me. I didn't want to look at it. I gave it back to her.

"You read it. Don't tell me what it says," I said.

She read it over. I studied her face carefully. The side of her mouth stretched slightly. It wasn't good. I felt sick.

"What does it say?" I asked.

"You told me not to tell you!"

"It's bad, isn't it? He's mad, isn't he?"

"Uh. I'd say so. He says 'Are you shitting me? You need to be an adult and learn to handle your parents better. This is fucking ridiculous'."

"Oh my God," I gasped and took the phone. She wasn't lying or sugar–coating it either. "Wha...what do I say? He hates me." I spat out the last words. The tears pinched behind my eyes, threatening to emerge again.

"What did you expect, Perry? I mean...he's kind of right."

I fastened my eyes on her, hoping her smug face would

burst into a million flames. She flinched a little and that same look I saw in my mother's eyes passed over hers. All the anger and bitterness from earlier was rising up from my throat. It wanted to come out and get her.

I closed my eyes tightly and tried to keep calm. I felt so disjointed. It was hard to get control of my thoughts and to keep reality in check. She was just being Ada; I should have known better than that. And Dex had every right to be mad. If he hated me, I could only just accept it. I was the only one to blame here.

There was so much shame inside me. So much that it scared me. I felt like I was heading down a big, deep hole again. Who would pull me out this time? I couldn't even trust myself to do it. I was a miserable, pathetic mess. No job. No show. No Dex.

"Are you OK?" Ada asked. I realized I had been off in my head, boring holes in her Zac Efron poster with my eyes. I wasn't sure how much time had passed but my knuckles were blue from gripping my phone.

I wasn't OK. Not in the slightest. I needed to either pass out and push the world go away, or embrace it and put on the angriest music I had. Since almost all of my music was angry rock and heavy metal, that wouldn't be a problem. NIN might do the trick. Then I would systematically trash my bedroom and maybe put a hole in my wall. I'd done it before.

"You know what," she said getting up. "I'm going to go make you some tea. Then we'll think of what to do next and stuff."

I nodded bleakly and laid my head down on her pillow.

CHAPTER THREE

The sound of the doorbell's jarring ring entered my dreams and eased me awake. Something about water, darkness, a baby crying. Then the fragments of the dream were gone. Where was I? My eyes focused lazily on the silky ribbon tails that were sticking out of Ada's desk drawer. She had won those years ago when she was a promising ballerina. *She must be ashamed of them now*, I thought absently.

I raised my head up higher and looked at her alarm clock. It was 8 p.m. There was a full cup of tea on the bedside. I must have fallen asleep while she made it for me.

I heard a sharp giggle and flipped over to see her sitting on her window seat, on the phone with someone. She was listening intently and smiling broadly, her cheeks pink. I immediately knew it was a boy.

My phone was lying beside me in bed and everything came flooding back to me. The fight with my parents, what Dex had said. As disappointed as I was to realize that it wasn't a dream, I was too exhausted, emotionally and physically, to care as much as I did earlier. My heart and head were heavy and even when I tried to think about everything that had changed, I was numb.

There was also a tiny bit of relief washing over me. That was the one bright side to all of this: I didn't have to lie anymore. That weight was no longer on my shoulders.

I eased myself up on my elbows and rubbed my temples. Naps always made me feel more tired than before I went to sleep, and this was definitely no exception.

"Yeah, it's OK," Ada said into the phone, her voice a few octaves higher than normal. "I should stay home. I don't think my parents would let me out anyway. They're stupid."

She burst into a flurry of girlish giggles before saying, "OK hottie, see you tomorrow. Bye."

She hung up her cell, staring at it for a few moments with a goofy grin on her face before placing it down beside her.

"Hottie? Who was that?" I asked groggily, not meaning to intrude but insanely curious just the same. I knew Ada liked guys, but I didn't recall her ever calling any of them "hottie" before.

I fully expected her to tell me to mind my own business but instead she rushed over to me and held out her pinky finger.

"Pinky swear you won't tell Mom and Dad?"

I took her pinky in my own and promised. For once Ada looked and sounded like someone I could relate to.

"Okaaay," she grinned and went over to her designer bag and started rifling through it. She pulled out a high school yearbook photo, you know the terrible ones you got to hand out to your friends and sign the back of. Not that many people ever wanted mine with my double chin and blue hair and all.

I took it and looked it over. The cute, albeit older, face of a buzz–cut boy stared back at me. He looked like a jock with nary a spark of intelligence behind his dull eyes.

"That's Layton. He's my boyfriend." She pronounced 'boyfriend' like it was joke. I could see from her eyes she wasn't joking though. She was head over heels and trying to play it cool.

"How long have you guys been dating?" I asked, feeling just a tad protective. I remembered last month I had found a box of condoms in her drawer (I wasn't snooping if that's what you think) and prayed she wasn't using it with this guy. He looked too old for her.

"Oh, since the beginning of the school year," she said in a tone that was both casual and proud.

"And he's a good kid?"

"Yes," she sighed, and snatched the photo out of my hands. "Are you Mom now?"

"I'm just wondering."

"You don't trust my judgment."

"I..." I put my hands up in the air and ended up shrugging. "He looks cute. I'm glad he makes you happy."

"He does," she squealed. "He's more than cute, he's fucking hot. And he's on like every sports team there is."

I never pegged Ada to be the type to think dating a jock was cool, but if it was popular, then that explained a lot. Ada operated a successful fashion blog and who knows how many people she won over on a daily basis from just showing off her enviable body and insane wardrobe.

I wonder if she gets any hateful blog comments, I thought. I made a mental note to ask her later.

The image of the condom box flashed in my head again. I had to say, "I hope you're not sleeping with him."

"Perry!" she admonished. "That's none of your business."

"Maybe not...and I don't want it to be. I just want you to be careful. Things can turn ugly really fast and if you're not careful..." Fuzzy, angry memories drifted into my head. I waved them away.

"I am careful!"

"So you are having sex!" I exclaimed.

She leaped off the bed and crossed her arms. "For your information, no I'm not. And like you're a saint...you're sleeping with Dex."

Now it was my time to leap off the bed. "I am not!"

The accusation was ludicrous (though immensely appealing).

She raised her penciled brow at me. "Right," she said slowly. "You just spend all this time with this 'hot' older guy, you know, being chased by ghosts or whatever and jetting all over the place. Sure you're not fucking him."

My jaw dropped. It all sounded so vulgar coming from her mouth. Suddenly I felt ashamed that I had those feelings to begin with. And why did she use air quotes around "hot"?

"First of all, Missy," I said, sticking up my fingers and ticking them off, "I'm 23–"

"22."

"Whatever. I'm 22. Which means I'm old enough to be able to handle having sex with someone. Second of all, Dex has a girlfriend. Third of all, Dex is my partner. Yes, we spend a lot of time together, but it's on a purely professional level."

More images flitted into my head while I was saying that. The way he sometimes looked at me, like he was searching deep inside my skull to discover how I was really feeling. The times I found myself being comforted in his arms. The way I had fallen asleep with my head on his bare chest, hearing his heartbeat lull me to sleep. The way his lips felt on my mouth, the jolt of electricity that made dying almost seem like a fair tradeoff.

"Yeah, well you obviously want to sleep with him and it's only a matter of time," she said, stuffing the photo back into her purse like it was a secret document.

My ears pricked up at that comment but I brushed it away. "I doubt it, Ada. It won't happen."

"I hope you're right," she said as she walked over to the

side table and picked up the cold mug of tea. "Do you want me to make you more tea since this went to waste?"

"Sure and what do you mean, you hope I'm right?"

"I'm sure you can figure it out," she said overconfidently and walked out of the room.

Figure it out? Figure what out?

I hopped off of her bed and followed her into the hallway like a curious cat. She had stopped halfway down the staircase and was just standing there, staring into the living room just as she had done earlier when I was fighting with my parents. A horrible feeling swept across me. What was she looking at? Were my parents both dead in the living room?

I didn't even let my mind dwell on that morbid thought. I walked down the stairs to join her and heard my dad's voice boom, "Just know I don't like this one bit," letting me know that they weren't dead after all.

I stopped beside my sister and followed her gaze.

My dad and mom were sitting in their armchairs. It was like they hadn't moved at all. The glass fragments and paintings were still on the floor.

They weren't alone. On the couch across from them was a man.

It took a few seconds to realize that I knew who the man was. I knew his slouchy position as he leaned forward on his cargo pants, his grey hoodie, his floppy, messy dark hair.

My nerves were on fire, gluing me to the spot. I wanted to look at Ada to see if she could see what I was seeing but I couldn't look away.

I closed my eyes tightly, thinking it was some fucked–up illusion. It wouldn't have been the first time.

When I opened them, the room had gone quiet and my parents were looking up at me. Dex slowly turned his head in my direction and our eyes met. Those eyes of his were unmistakable. Dex was in my living room, talking with my parents.

What. The. Fuck?

I was speechless. And thoughtless. I could only stand there, staring. I'm pretty sure my mouth was agape too.

"Perry, seems you have a visitor," my mother said.

I barely heard her. My eyes were still locked with Dex's. They were masked and offered no clues to what was going on. But the tiniest twitch of his upper lip said enough.

Out of the corner of my eye I became aware that Ada was watching me closely. Everyone was waiting for me to say something.

So I said the first thing that came to my mind. "Dex... what are you doing here?"

He pursed his lips and let it slide. He casually looked at my dad, who had stood up.

"Dex came all the way over here from Seattle to talk business. Your business," Dad said in that command respect sort of way. It was the professor in him coming out.

I finally looked at Ada. Her eyes were wide but she seemed to be enjoying the whole situation.

Dex was looking at us. He got up, easing himself off the couch, and sauntered over to the staircase, eyeing Ada with a bemused smirk."This must be Little Fifteen."

"The name's Ada," she said in her angsty teen voice, the amusement disappearing from her face. "You must be Perry's crazy partner. You're a lot shorter than I thought you'd be."

I closed my eyes in embarrassment while Dex said, "Ah. I can already tell you guys are related. The Snarky Sisters."

I opened my eyes at that just in time to see Ada muster the evilest stink eye as she flounced down the stairs and went into the kitchen. I looked back down at Dex.

"Sorry to just show up unannounced. Can we talk?" he asked in that rich voice of his. I glanced over his head at my parents. They seemed to expect it. I don't know what they had been talking about but it was obvious Dex needed to bring me up to speed in private.

I nodded and looked up the stairs. My bedroom seemed like the most obvious place. I could almost feel Ada snickering in the kitchen at how absurd (and fitting) the situation had gotten in the last few minutes, from talking about how I hadn't slept with Dex, to leading him to my bedroom. It was insanity.

I walked up them with Dex coming up behind me. I felt shaky, nervous and pale. I wasn't prepared for this. I could almost feel the energy he radiated glowing at my back. Then vanity kicked in. Was my bedroom clean? Did I have underwear flung all over the place? I must have looked like absolute shit from crying my eyes out.

I opened my door. The desk lamp was already on but that light was a bit too romantic so I flipped on the overhead lights and ushered Dex inside. He stopped in the middle of the room and looked around, taking it all in. I closed the door behind us and did a quick scan to make sure nothing was out of the ordinary.

It was messy as usual but my underwear and embarrassing items were tucked away for once. Well, I guess the row of stuffed animals I had could have counted as embarrassing. Least they were when he laughed and lazed over to them, picking up my tattered monkey Tim.

He waved it in my direction. "How old is this poor guy? His fucking eye is hanging out." He flicked it with his finger and it waved back and forth like a pendulum.

I gasped and ran over, plucking Tim out of his destructive hands. "That's Tim and I've had him since I was two years old." I held Tim to my chest in protective instinct. Dex stared at me with utter amusement.

"So I have stuffed animals, so what?" I asked defensively. I thought my Alice in Chains and Melvins posters made up for that fact.

He smiled, shrugged. I put Tim back down in the pile with the rest of his friends.

"So?" I asked, turning around to face him, feeling all nervy again.

He was looking over my walls. "So what?" he repeated blankly.

I reached over and smacked him lightly on his shoulder so his focus was on me.

"Dex. What are you doing here?"

He frowned. "You're not happy to see me?"

My head craned back on my neck, caught off guard. "Well, yeah, but...I mean..."

"It's OK, I won't hold it against you. Unless you want me to."

I raised my brow.

He grinned, a very quick flash, before he wiped it off with the back of his hand. Then he was all serious, his lips in a tight line.

"I couldn't let you back out of the show," he admitted. "I knew if you talked to your parents you'd just fuck it all up even more."

I winced. That wasn't very nice. But Dex was nothing if not brutally honest at times.

"It's just a two–hour drive," he continued, oblivious. "I've done more for a lot less."

"You should have told me," I said.

"Yeah? And have you freaking out for the next two hours? Come on, kiddo, I think I know you by now. This way was easier. And it worked. You can thank me, by the way."

"What do you mean, it worked?"

He walked over to my bed, humming some song to himself. He lied down on it, putting his hands behind his head and kicked the mattress with the back of his heel. "Not bad, not bad. Could be a bit bigger, though. How do you fit your boyfriends on here?"

As annoying as he was being, it was a nice change to see him being a little more playful than the last time I saw him. Still, I didn't want him to get the wrong idea and I wanted to be a little bit serious about the situation. I went over to my chair, pulled it over to him and sat down.

"Dex. What did you talk about with my parents? What was the business?"

"Oh," he said as if he was surprised. "I just told your father that you'd be in some legal trouble if you broke your contract."

My jaw opened a little bit.

"Uh, you have some balls, you know that?"

"Oh, I know." He grinned to himself.

"I'm serious. That's like...that's like threatening my father. My father does not take threats well. Believe me."

Dex looked at me, turning his head to the side. "You give your parents too much credit. Your dad is just a dude. He may be your big, scary father but to me he's just a man who likes his wine, indulges in hypocrisy on a daily basis, and does what he can to be the main provider of the house. He responded just like I thought he would, like any man would. To reason. To logic. If you backed out of the contract, ShowNet would take action. You can't break it without just cause and the fact that you haven't figured out how to have a proper relationship with your parents is not just cause. Sometimes you need someone on the outside to point out common sense."

I mulled that over with a mix of emotions. I didn't like how Dex assumed he knew my parents better than I did, and I didn't appreciate his condescending opinion on our relationship. He knew nothing about me and my parents – he hadn't been here, growing up in this house, dealing with all the shit we had to deal with. But on the other hand...it worked.

I didn't feel like giving him credit though.

"And then..." I coaxed him.

"What? He agreed. He gave me some big long spiel about how disappointed he was in you and how he raised you better than that, which I tried not to laugh at, and how this show was not a proper career and blah, blah, blah–"

"Yeah, I've heard enough of that today, thank you."

"But then he came around and said it was only professional to do the right thing. Which is to keep doing the show. But you're going to have to start paying rent here. Sorry about that."

"What!?" I yelled, the loudness of my own voice surprising me. It didn't surprise Dex, though. He only looked mildly apologetic.

"You're 22. You probably *should* start paying rent. I have to pay my mortgage. It's called being an adult. Responsibility."

My fists began to clench again. I'd have a heart attack by the time this dreadful day was over.

"Thanks for the lecture, Dex. I turn 23 next week."

He chuckled. "That's not helping your case."

I sighed angrily and walked over to my dresser. I spotted

a vial of this herbal remedy you sprayed in your mouth every time you were upset or about to have a panic attack. It was probably all a placebo effect but that didn't matter if it worked, did it? It was almost empty.

I sprayed it into my mouth as Dex got off of the bed and sauntered over to me, curiosity flickering in his eyes.

"Breath freshener?" he asked, taking it from my hands and reading the label over. He looked disbelieving and gave it back to me. "You've had quite the day, haven't you?"

"How can you tell?" I muttered sarcastically.

"It's written all over your face," he said pointing at my eyes. "Those bags belong in cargo hold."

I gave him my most withering look. "Did you come here to make things better or make things worse?"

I aimed the spray into my mouth but the nozzle was turned the other way.

I ended up squirting Dex right in the face.

He winced hard, grunted and turned away. I swear it was an accident but it was a perfect one. I burst into giggles.

He wiped his watering eyes and stepped backward.

"I guess I deserved that," he said, blinking rapidly at me. "What's in this, pure alcohol? No wonder it calms you down."

He came forward again and rested his hand on my shoulder. I felt that warm current flowing between us.

"Look, kiddo, I saved your ass," he grimaced, wiping away a tear.

"It's a pretty big ass."

The smile came easily to his lips, his eyes red but dancing. "We both know how I feel about your ass."

Ah, yes. He had grabbed it while we were slow dancing at the bar in Red Fox. It was the first time anyone had complimented my bubble butt. Well, anyone of importance, that is. And just like that I was starting to get inappropriate thoughts, images and feelings in my head, swimming around in a heady circle.

And the reality, that he was in my bedroom, standing close to me, his hand on my shoulder, wasn't helping matters either. I became aware that I hadn't said anything and the silence was getting awkward.

I cleared my throat. "I'm thankful you saved my ass. I really am."

He squeezed my shoulder. I stared up at his face, his strong jaw and expressively wide mouth flanked by his barely there 'stache, his low, dark brow that sheltered those all–knowing eyes that shined like polished coffee, the way his black hair flopped lazily across his handsome forehead. Wow. Thoughts like that weren't helping the awkwardness either.

He's your partner you idiot, I told myself. I broke my study of him and focused on the rescue spray in my hands. "So we're still on for this weekend?"

With his hand still on my shoulder he said, "How about right now?"

"What?"

"How fast can you pack?"

"Sorry, you didn't answer my 'what?'" I wasn't supposed to be ready until Friday.

Finally he took his hand off of me. My shoulder felt cold and exposed without his comforting palm. He walked over to my closet and flung it open.

"It's just as nineties as I thought," he said to himself, inspecting the haphazard contents. "Should I just start grab-bing stuff? You kind of wear the same thing every day. Let's see, we need leggings, a band t–shirt and skirt. Maybe jeans."

I marched over to him and shut my closet door, facing him with my arms held against it like I was guarding some secret passage. "Seriously, where could we possibly be going tonight? Also, I wear my band shirts to sleep."

"I've seen you wear them at other times. Weren't you wearing a Kings of Leon shirt last week?"

"Dex!" I said through gritted teeth. I hated KOL with a passion. And also, he was pissing me off with his avoidance.

He yawned. Don't tell me he was bored?

"Here's the plan. I drove all the way down here to, uh, fix things. Now it makes perfect sense that you come up with me tonight to Vancouver. BC. Canada. Not the fake Vancouver across the river."

"Are you kidding me?" I said. "It's like nine o'clock at night!"

"OK, maybe we won't make it as far as Vancouver, but anyway, we'll get as far as we can. We have a hockey game to attend!"

"What?" I rubbed my temples again. None of this was making any sense.

"You said last time that it would be 'great' if we actually hung out in a normal setting and got to know each other as people instead of running around with ghosts and scaring our panties off each other."

It's true. I did say that. Not the panties part but I did mention, offhand by the way, that it would be nice if we could just hang out like normal people did. Like friends. But I didn't see where this was going.

He read the confusion on my face. It wasn't hard. "There's a Canucks hockey game against the Rangers tomorrow night. I got us tickets. We have to go to Vancouver anyway, to talk to someone about the filming. So you know, I was just trying to be a good guy and please you."

"Phhff," I sniffed. "Please me? What if I said I hated hockey?"

"I'd never speak to you again," he said, narrowing his eyes. It was hard to see how serious he was. He hadn't really mentioned hockey before, at least not when I was listening, but he also took the weirdest things very seriously. "Is it true?"

"No." I didn't have anything against the sport, I just didn't know anything about hockey. Understandable, since we had no NHL teams in Oregon, just the minor league Portland Winterhawks.

"Good," he said, still watching me carefully. "Then we can still be friends."

"So, we leave tonight…go to the island on Friday?"

"Correct–a–mundo. Then we come back on Sunday, just in time for your birthday on Monday."

"You know when my birthday is?" I was sorta touched by that. It was sad that I was so easily impressed.

He tapped his head. "I'm more observant than you think. Now, without any more jerking off from you, I suggest you get packing as fast as you can. I'll help. Where are your bras and underwear?"

I rolled my eyes, pulled out my overnight bag and started cramming crap in there.

I don't think I've ever packed so fast in my life – I obviously needed to get out of that house more than I knew.

With Dex at my side it also kept any exchanges with my parents at a polite distance. My dad even helped us rummage through the garage to find me a sleeping bag. Staying on the island did not involve staying in any fancy cabins. We would be camping the entire time. Yeah, in November. In Canada. Fun times.

I could tell my parents were having a hard time coming to terms with the situation. They were still mad at my lies, disappointed in my choices but at the same time they understood where Dex was coming from. As much as they hated the idea that I had involved another person in my problem, they had no choice but to accept it. And having Dex there, an accomplished (sorta) and mature (again, sorta) man there probably helped.

And Ada...well, I knew how Ada felt about the whole thing. Just as we were coming out of the garage, she yanked me aside.

"You're totally going to sleep with him now," she hissed roughly in my ear.

I ignored her. There was no way I was going to get caught in that argument again, not with the subject slinking around in front of me.

Luckily we made it out of the house in record time and were soon cruising through the darkness on the I–5, heading north. Dex's black Highlander was packed with everything from filmmaking equipment to a tent and camping gear.

Dex is one of those people who prefers to blast the music loudly and keep chit–chat down to a minimum. This trip was no exception. I found a strange comfort in our shared silence now, just hearing the music and the sound of his toothpick as it flitted against his teeth. When we first met I was so nervous being alone with him, I just needed to blab about anything to fill the air. I felt just a teeny bit proud that I knew Dex enough now that if we needed to talk, he'd be the one bringing it up.

Which is what happened an hour into our journey. I

was in the midst of checking my emails on my phone when I felt him give me a curious look. It sounds stupid but you can always tell when Dex is looking at you. At least I could, even from miles away. Something about those eyes...

"So I've seen you've got your fair share of haters on the blog already," he said. "Good job."

I sighed loudly. I had wanted to talk about this for so long.

"You're telling me," I said, giving him a pained and drawn–out look.

He seemed to think on that for a moment; a hint of gentleness graced his expression.

"Well, that's the nature of the internet," he mused matter–of–factly. "If you didn't have haters, then I'd worry."

"Yeah but they are really mean," I pointed out.

"The internet is full of meanies. Their opinion doesn't matter."

Yes, it does, I thought.

He picked up on that. "Okay, it shouldn't matter."

"Maybe we should close down the comment section... it reflects badly on the show, doesn't it?"

He chuckled to himself and shook his head. "No can do, kiddo. Don't underestimate the power of creating a community on the web. By having a place for people to voice their opinion, no matter how fucked it is, attracts more people to the site. The more people to the site, the more people to watch the show, the more people to watch the show, the more ads we get, the more ads we get, the more pay I get, and eventually you. It's a numbers game. You just have to buck up and ignore the haters. Everyone gets them, from the smallest blogs to the biggest websites."

"Besides," he said, slapping me on the leg. "I think it'll be good for you. Toughen you up a bit."

"I'm already tough enough," I muttered.

"If you were that tough, this wouldn't be bothering you. It should be water right off your back."

My eyes automatically narrowed into two little slits. He took his eyes off the road and smiled when he saw them. Not the response I was going for.

"Is that look supposed to scare me?" he asked, his lips twitching in amusement.

I wanted to explode on him, just start shooting the salvos and bring up a lot of crap about my past, so he had an actual idea what it was like to be me. But I couldn't. Because what he said actually had a point to it. I always considered myself tough...going through drugs and other problems while in high school, growing up with a family shrink (all my doing), the stunt woman classes I had taken for a defunct career. I had been through a lot – mentally and physically. So how was it that a few comments from people I didn't know were weighing on my mind so much?

I kept my mouth shut and looked out the window at the black rushes of roadside that flew past.

"Honestly," he spoke in a more serious tone. "It's not worth your time, Perry. You're better than that. And the more successful this gets, the more successful you get...it's only going to get worse. But you'll be OK."

At that last bit he reached over for me again, but instead of slapping my leg, he squeezed my knee. It was borderline ticklish. Any more pressure and I would have been squirming. He didn't remove it right away, either, and I could feel his eyes coaxing mine to meet them.

Too many feelings were running through me and my body was responding; my tongue felt dry and thick, the skin on my upper neck danced nervously, the hairs coming alive. I looked at him. He seemed concerned or interested in my response but there was something else lurking behind those brown eyes. Something I couldn't place my finger on. It was almost as if he was undecided. A restlessness.

"So where are we staying tonight? Your place?" I found myself saying.

At that his eyes flinched and he quickly withdrew his hand.

"No," he said, pursing his lips. I obviously said the wrong thing. I wanted to push it.

"Does Jenn object?"

If he flinched it was barely detectable. He did crunch down hard on his toothpick before saying, "No, no. She...it's just better if we get as close to Vancouver as possible. I think Bellingham is probably a safe bet, just find a Motel 6 there or something like that. If we went through the border now we'd cause too much of a fuss...especially with all the gear back there. I don't want to tell them we're there on work since we would need a visa and all that."

I nodded, not really convinced by his spiel but it did make sense. I wouldn't have blamed Jenn anyway if she didn't want me in their apartment. Still, the apprehension that Dex subtly gave off was enough to make me store the memory in my mind for future use. There was something else, and maybe one day I'd figure it out.

....finish the rest by picking up Dead Sky Morning!

ABOUT THE AUTHOR

Karina Halle, a former screenwriter, travel writer and music journalist, is the *New York Times, Wall Street Journal,* and *USA Today* bestselling author of *The Pact, A Nordic King,* and *Sins & Needles,* as well as over fifty other wild and romantic reads. She, her husband, and their adopted pit bull live in a rain forest on an island off British Columbia, where they operate a B&B that's perfect for writers' retreats. In the winter, you can often find them in California or on their beloved island of Kauai, soaking up as much sun (and getting as much inspiration) as possible. For more information, visit

www.authorkarinahalle.com

ALSO BY KARINA HALLE

Contemporary Romances

Love, in English

Love, in Spanish

Where Sea Meets Sky (from Atria Books)

Racing the Sun (from Atria Books)

The Pact

The Offer

The Play

Winter Wishes

The Lie

The Debt

Smut

Heat Wave

Before I Ever Met You

After All

Rocked Up

Wild Card (North Ridge #1)

Maverick (North Ridge #2)

Hot Shot (North Ridge #3)

Bad at Love

The Swedish Prince

The Wild Heir

A Nordic King

Nothing Personal

My Life in Shambles

Discretion

Disarm

Disavow

The Royal Rogue

The Forbidden Man

Lovewrecked

One Hot Italian Summer

The One That Got Away

All the Love in the World (Anthology)

Romantic Suspense Novels by Karina Halle

Sins and Needles (The Artists Trilogy #1)

On Every Street (An Artists Trilogy Novella #0.5)

Shooting Scars (The Artists Trilogy #2)

Bold Tricks (The Artists Trilogy #3)

Dirty Angels (Dirty Angels #1)

Dirty Deeds (Dirty Angels #2)

Dirty Promises (Dirty Angels #3)

Black Hearts (Sins Duet #1)

Dirty Souls (Sins Duet #2)

Horror Romance

Darkhouse (EIT #1)

Red Fox (EIT #2)

The Benson (EIT #2.5)

Dead Sky Morning (EIT #3)

Lying Season (EIT #4)

On Demon Wings (EIT #5)

Old Blood (EIT #5.5)

The Dex-Files (EIT #5.7)

Into the Hollow (EIT #6)

And With Madness Comes the Light (EIT #6.5)

Come Alive (EIT #7)

Ashes to Ashes (EIT #8)

Dust to Dust (EIT #9)

Ghosted (EIT #9.5)

Came Back Haunted (EIT #10)

The Devil's Duology

Donners of the Dead

Veiled